Kevin's Wish

A Christmas Novella

Debbie Williams

Prologue

Bethesda, Maryland

Lexi Carter walked down the long corridor of the hospital checking door numbers along the way. As she neared the number that she was looking for, she saw two women that she recognized speaking quietly in the hall. They stopped talking and looked solemnly at her as she approached them.

"Hi," Lexi said to them. "Have you seen him? How is he?"

"We saw him," the younger of the two women told her. "He is in a lot of pain. It is … hard to see." Her tone was not exactly welcoming.

Kevin's Wish

Lexi stared at Greg's sister. Even at a time like this, her mind once again asked the question, "Why does this woman have such a dislike for me?"

The older of the two women gave her a small smile. "He has been asking for you. Go on in and see him."

Lexi returned the smile to Greg's mother and stepped past the two of them before she opened the door. As she entered the room, she couldn't help but notice that the lights were very dim. With the small amount of light and all of the medical equipment that was in the room, it took a moment for her to focus on the bed in the corner.

She walked across the room and looked down at the man lying in the bed. Fortunately, his eyes were closed so he could not see what must have been a look of shock on her face. This man did not resemble the man that she had hugged so hard just a few weeks ago, right before his unit deployed to Afghanistan. He seemed so thin and there was very little color in his face.

After a moment, she spoke softly. "Greg?"

He seemed to struggle to open his eyes, and then it took a few more seconds for him to be able to focus on her. Then, as he recognized her, he smiled just a little.

Lex leaned down and kissed him on top of the forehead.

"Did they tell you?" he asked in a groggy voice.

"Yes," she answered. "I know that you lost a leg, but you are alive. I would rather have you here with me, missing a leg, than have to go to your funeral. It won't be easy, but we will get through this together."

He was quiet for a moment and then he looked up at her and spoke in a choked voice.

"No, Lex, we won't."

"What do you mean?" she asked.

"We won't get through this together," he continued. "I love you, but you deserve more than a cripple like me."

"I don't understand," she said. "Don't talk like that."

"Do you love me?" he asked.

"You know I do," she said.

"Then you should honor my wishes." He paused and then took a breath. "I want you to go home and don't come back. Start a new life and move on from me."

"Greg, no! Please don't say that!"

"Lex, my mind is made up. Please just turn around and walk out of here."

"Honey, have you forgotten that…"

"I said, GO!".

"Greg…what about?"

"Now!"

Lexi then watched in horror as he picked up the metal bedpan from the nightstand and threw it across the room with all of his might. It hit the wall with a resounding clang and then crashed loudly on the floor. A deafening silence then filled the room.

She looked at his face one more time and the darkness and despair that she saw in his eyes frightened her to the core of her soul. Not knowing what else to do, she turned and fled out the door, where she nearly knocked Greg's sister and mother over as she began to run down the hall. Passing the elevator completely, she yanked open the door to the stairway and began to descend the steps rapidly. Ten minutes later, she was sitting on a bench somewhere in Bethesda, Maryland, crying her eyes out, wondering what she was going to do.

Chapter One

Six Years Later

Brookline, Massachusetts

Lexi sat across the desk, from Paul Fletcher, her beloved boss and the one father figure in her life.

"I don't want to alarm you in any way, Lexi," he began, "but I just want you to know that the enrollment of students attending classes here at this campus and at the main campus is down. I believe that this is directly correlated to the rise in students taking our online courses."

"Are you saying that you think this campus is going to close?" she asked him.

Paul thought for a moment before he responded. "Not immediately," he answered, "I do want you to know, however, that as long as I hold a position as the Dean here, you will have a job as my secretary and assistant. I do plan to work for one more year before I retire, and by then I am not sure how much longer the university will fund this small campus."

She sighed a small sigh of relief. She had a job at least for the immediate future.

"I do think, however, that you should be alert to any possibilities of jobs that might present themselves to you," he said. "I certainly wouldn't want you to feel any loyalty to me if an opportunity were to come your way."

"I appreciate that," she told him. "Maybe it is time for me to start doing some research to see what's available."

"That might be a good idea," he answered. "Now what time can we expect our little guest tomorrow?"

Lexi smiled. It wasn't easy raising a five-year-old alone while holding down a full-time job, but Paul and his wife were a blessing to her.

"I really appreciate you giving up your Saturday evening to watch Kevin. I hadn't planned to go to Jill's wedding, but when she called me last month in a panic because one of her bridesmaids had broken her leg, I just couldn't say no."

"The wedding is in Quincy?" he asked.

"Yes," she answered. "It's only about twenty minutes away. Jill is a longtime friend of mine. She asked me about bringing Kevin to the wedding and when I told her that I had already made arrangements for him, she insisted that I bring him to the rehearsal tonight. That won't be a problem, but I will need to be at the venue tomorrow by one. I could have taken him, but it would have been a terribly long and boring day for him."

Paul laughed. "It certainly would have."

"I was planning to drop him off around noon, if that's all right?"

"That will be just fine," he told her. "Val is really looking forward to this. Now, are you still all right with him spending the night?"

Lexi sighed. "The only other time that I have spent the night away from him was when I had my appendix out and my sister kept him. Since she moved to Georgia, it has been just the two of us. I trust you and Val, though. I'm sure he will be fine. I have no idea how late I will be, so this will be for the best."

"Your mother doesn't come back here for visits, does she?"

"No," Lexi answered. "She does not. Every Christmas and every summer, she buys us plane tickets so we can visit her. Since Dad's death three years ago, she has created a whole new world for herself in Florida. I think there are just too many painful memories here."

Paul did not respond, but only nodded. At that point the phone rang, and Lexi went to her desk to answer it.

Kevin's Wish

That night after returning from the rehearsal, Lexi had a difficult time settling herself to sleep. The wedding activities had brought out memories and emotions from the past that she had not expected.

She sat up and switched on the lamp by her bed and stared at the navy-blue formal gown hanging on the door across the room. Hugging her knees, she thought of her own small wedding just a few years ago. Although it had been a brief ceremony, it had been very special. She and Greg had then spent five wonderful days alone together before he had shipped out. They had made a decision that they would not tell anyone about their marriage until he returned from Afghanistan. Other than her family and the Fletchers, she had not told one living soul that she and Greg were married. Her name was legally changed to Carter, but that was a secret that she managed to keep, with very little difficulty.

After Kevin's birth, she had put Greg's name on the birth certificate as the father and had given Kevin the last name of Carter. When he had gotten old enough to question where his father was, she had simply told him that his father's job was in the army and he worked far away. That had worked well, until recently when Kevin's questions were becoming more difficult to answer. He was in kindergarten now and had friends who had fathers. She knew in her heart that she was going to have to make some difficult decisions in the near future.

To the best of her knowledge, Greg had no idea of Kevin's existence. She realized that this was not fair, but he had been the one that had sent her away. Her original plan that horrible day in Bethesda was to tell him about the pregnancy in hopes that he would be inspired to work hard to recover from his injuries. After he demanded that she leave in such a violent manner, she had been frightened away.

A month after the birth of their son, she had attempted to contact Greg. His phone had been disconnected and then she had made several efforts to call his mother. The messages that she had left were not returned. A very short time later, that number was also disconnected. Finally, she had tried to call his sister. The call went unanswered and then she received a text message from her stating that Greg's mother had passed away and that he was having a very difficult time with his grief and his physical recovery. It went on to ask her to please leave them alone and not bring further stress into their lives. After Lexi recovered from the shock of the news, she attempted to send a condolence text, only to find that that number had also been changed.

At one point, she did contact an online attorney about an annulment and learned that she could get the paperwork from the courthouse, but she would need to locate Greg, and get his signature. After considerable thought, she decided not to pursue the issue. Kevin was her son and somehow it seemed right to be married to his father. Greg knew that they were married. If he wanted out, he would have to find her. That had settled the matter for the time being, but Kevin's ongoing curiosity and his almost daily new questions were bringing the issue to the forefront.

The next day at the venue, Lexi forced herself to enjoy all of the festivities. Just before it was time to walk down the aisle, she took one last look in the mirror. She smiled and realized that it had been a long time since she had been this dressed up. Her long ash blonde hair was down and curled into cascades across her shoulders. The deep blue of the dress brought out the grey in her eyes, along with the professional makeup work that the bride had provided. The dress fit nicely and showed that she still had a nice figure in spite of the weight she had gained and lost with the birth of Kevin. Her life at this time offered little reason to get dressed up, but it was nice to know that she could still pull it off if she wanted to.

Twenty minutes later, she was the first bridesmaid to walk down the aisle. She took her place at the end of the row and watched the other girls walk down and take their places in the front. Shortly after Jill made her way down to the front, the ceremony began. Lexi listened to the minister and watched as the couple held hands and vowed to love one another forever.

While the rings were being exchanged, for some unknown reason, Lexi looked out at the guests seated in the church pews in front of her. She had to stop herself from gasping when she saw who was sitting about five rows back. It had been almost six years since she had seen Greg, but the sight of him still made her heart lurch. He looked much more like his old self than he did the last time she had seen him. He was watching the ceremony intently with a small smile on his face. Then without warning, he looked up at her and their eyes locked. Lexi froze, not sure what to expect. She was a little surprised and a little relieved when he smiled at her. She couldn't help but smile back at him and then suddenly the music began, and the newly married couple started to walk up the aisle.

A few minutes later, Lexi found herself outside in the receiving line greeting guests. It wasn't long before she could see Greg about five people away working his way through the line.

When he did reach her, he greeted her like an old friend; taking her hand and kissing her on the cheek.

"It's good to see you Lex," he said. "You look fantastic."

"Thank you," she answered. "You look well too. How are you doing?"

"I'm doing great," he told her. He seemed to want to say something else, but he looked over his shoulder and saw the line waiting behind him. "I'll see you at the reception," he said and moved on.

The next two hours passed in a frenzy of photo shoots, introductions and a catered dinner.

Lexi did not cross paths with Greg again until after the cake cutting. She was in the back hallway waiting in line for the restroom when he came out of the men's room. When he saw her, he stopped and turned around before taking a few steps toward her.

"Brian told me that you were going to be here tonight," he began. "I was glad to hear that. I've got something that I need to talk to you about."

She caught her breath because she wasn't sure where he was going with this, so she didn't say anything, but waited for him to continue.

He looked around at other people passing through the hallway. "I guess this isn't the time or place," he said. "Could we...."

"Hey Greg," a man's voice called from the end of the hallway. "We are all going to take a shot with Brian."

He sighed. "I'll catch up with you again before I leave. Ok?"

"Sure," she answered, watching him head down the hall. It occurred to her as he walked away that she didn't even detect a limp.

Kevin's Wish

In another hour and a half, the reception began to wind down. Lexi and a couple of the other bridesmaids began to carry the center pieces to the back of the venue so that they could be loaded into Jill's mother's car. On her third trip to the back, she was stopped by Greg.

"I'm getting ready to leave," he told her. "I was wondering...where are you living now?"

"I am living in Brookline," she said.

"That's not far," he answered. "I am living in Hull. I think it's only about an hour's drive. Would you be willing to meet with me tomorrow...maybe for brunch?"

She hesitated for a moment. "In Brookline?" she asked.

He nodded. "I have something I need to ask you about."

"I guess that would be all right," she said. "There is an IHOP right in town. Would you like to meet there about ten tomorrow morning?"

He nodded and then reached in his shirt pocket and pulled out a card which he handed to her. She took it and looked at it. It was a business card.

Carter Woodworks.

Handcrafted Furniture

On the other side it listed an address in Hull and a phone number.

"You are building furniture?" she asked.

He nodded. "I am doing quite well with it."

She smiled. "That's nice. I remember how you always loved to work with your hands."

He pulled another card and a pen out of his pocket. "Can I have your number, just in case I need to call you?"

Lexi looked at him and then gave him the number. After writing it down he said, "It's the same number."

"Yes," she said. "It is."

He smiled at her and then put the card and the pen back in his pocket. "I'll see you tomorrow morning then?"

She nodded and said, "Good night Greg."

"Good night Lex," he said as he headed toward the door.

She watched him walk out the door and then turned back to gathering centerpieces. She managed to keep all of the questions swirling in her head contained until she was on her way home. She called the Fletchers to check on Kevin. Val reported that he had had a wonderful evening. Paul had taught him how to play checkers and he had gone to bed a happy little boy. Lexi was relieved to hear that. She then explained that she had run into an old friend that invited her to brunch in the morning and asked if it would be all right if she didn't come to get him until noon. Val said that it was not a problem. She had promised Kevin a big waffle breakfast so that would be just fine.

With that issue dealt with, Lexi began to focus on the big question that was looming over head. "What did Greg want to talk to her about?"

"Did he want out of the marriage?"

"Had he found out about Kevin?"

Lexi spent a restless night worrying about how to handle the situation. She knew in her heart that the time had come for her to face her fears. She had to tell Greg about Kevin. There was no getting around it. It wasn't fair to him or to Kevin for her to keep this to herself any longer. The window of opportunity had presented itself and she couldn't ignore it any longer.

She arrived at the IHOP before Kevin. She had just started her second cup of coffee when he walked in. As she watched him work his way through the restaurant toward her, two things occurred to her. The first was that once again she noticed how smoothly he walked. The second was that he seemed to be every bit the same man that she had fallen in love with ten years ago.

He slid in the booth across from her and smiled. "Good morning, Lex"

She smiled back. "Good morning."

Shortly after that the waitress appeared, and they decided to go ahead and order. For the next half hour, they made small talk. He asked her about living in Brookline and her job. She asked him about his furniture business. He told her that the business and teaching a couple of classes at the local vocational school kept him busy. They discussed their parents. He told her how sorry he was to hear about her father's death, and she expressed her condolences about his mother.

Eventually, they finished their food and the waitress cleared away their dishes. After their coffee cups were refilled, Greg took a breath and leaned forward slightly. Lexi sensed that he had decided that the time had come to broach the subject of what he had asked to meet with her about. She took a sip of her coffee and waited.

"Lex," he began, "when you came to see me in the hospital in Bethesda right after I got back, I was in a very dark place. I...have a vague memory of what happened that day, but between what I remember and what my sister and mother told me, I know I was pretty horrible to you. I just want to..." He hesitated before he continued. "I am really sorry about that. I know that I hurt you very badly that day."

She didn't respond because she was trying to keep control of her emotions.

"I was being given a lot of pain killers and who knows what else. They told me that those kinds of medications sometimes mess with your memories; even of things that happened before you begin taking them. I am just now beginning to regain memories of the few weeks I was in Afghanistan." He stopped again and sighed.

"What I want to ask you about was time leading up to my deployment," he said. "I now remember that you and I went on some sort of trip just before I shipped out. What I want to ask you about is whether I am remembering that correctly. Did we take a trip, possibly up north? Maybe to Maine?"

Lexi stared at him and suddenly something became clear to her. Greg had no idea that they were married. He didn't remember!

After a moment she nodded. "Yes, we did. We went to Portland for about five days."

He returned her stare. Then she could see him bracing himself to ask the next question. "Did we get married?"

She looked him directly in the eye. "Yes, we did."

Greg let out the breath that he was holding. Another moment passed before he posed the next question. "Are we still married?"

"Yes," she answered. "We are."

Then there was a long moment of silence, as he seemed to be turning this news over in his mind. Eventually, he posed another question to her.

"In all this time, you never attempted to do anything about it?"

She shook her head.

"Why not?" he asked.

Her heart lurched, because she realized that the moment had come.

She took a deep breath and began, "Greg, there is something…"

The waitress suddenly appeared and interrupted their conversation, "Can I get you all something else? Some more coffee?"

"No thank you," Greg answered. "I'm good."

"No thank you," she said.

"You all have a nice day then," the waitress told them as she laid the check on the table.

Lexi looked toward the entrance at the line of people waiting for a seat. "Let's get out of here," she said. "I think we need to finish this conversation in private."

Fifteen minutes later, they were sitting in his truck in the parking lot. Greg was looking at her expectantly. Lexi could tell that he sensed that what she was about to say was important.

"You have something to tell me?" he asked.

She drew in another breath and began again. "The day I came to the hospital in Bethesda, I had something to tell you."

"Something important, I gather?"

She nodded. "I was going to tell you that I was pregnant. I guess I was naïve about the situation. I was convinced that the news would give you reason to work hard at your recovery."

Greg did not respond. He only stared at her, so she continued. "After you...threw me out, I...didn't know what to do. I went home to Medford and stayed with my sister. Between her and my parents, I managed to get by until I gave birth to a boy five years ago last May. Two years ago, I got the job at the college and moved to Brookline.

Kevin's Wish

I know that you are probably wondering why I would not let you know about something that important. I did try. About a month after I gave birth, I tried to call you. Your number was no longer in service, so I began attempting to call your mother. I left quite a few messages, and then suddenly that number was disconnected. I even tried to contact your sister. Again, my messages were ignored, until I received a text from her. She informed me that your mother had died and that you were not doing well. Then she kindly invited me to leave you alone. Shortly after that, her number was also disconnected. I didn't know what to do so I just focused on taking care of Kevin."

"You named him Kevin?" he asked. "After my father?"

"I did," she answered. "We always planned to name our first son, Kevin, after him."

It was quiet in the truck for a few minutes. Lexi sat with tears running quietly down her cheeks. Greg sat staring out the window and she had no idea what he was thinking.

Eventually she spoke again. "I know it's a lot to wrap your mind around."

He turned and looked at her. "What have you told him about me?"

"I told him that you were in the army and that you were working far away. He has accepted that until recently. He is in kindergarten now, and he has friends who have fathers, so he is beginning to see that their fathers are around. This is something that I have been wrestling with lately, so last night when I looked up and saw you sitting there, I just knew that I had to tell you. Then you said that you wanted to talk to me, so here we are."

"Where is he now?" he asked.

Lexi frowned. "He lives with me."

"What I meant was, where is he *right* now?"

"Oh," she said. "I work for Dean Fletcher at the college. He is with him and his wife. I called them on the way home last night and told them that I ran into an old friend that had invited me to brunch."

Suddenly a thought occurred to her and she pulled out her phone. She punched a few buttons and handed the phone to him.

"His first day of school pictures," she told him.

Greg spent the next few minutes wordlessly going through pictures on her phone.

When he finally handed the phone back to her, she could see that his eyes were misting.

"He is the spitting image of his father, isn't he?"

He nodded. "Can I see him?" he asked in somewhat of a hoarse voice.

She was surprised by the question. "Of course you can meet your son. Nothing would make me or him happier."

The following Saturday afternoon Lexi set off in her car to Hull, Massachusetts. During the entire hour-long ride, Kevin barraged her with endless questions about his father.

"Is he tall?" Yes.

"Does he look like me?" Yes.

"Does he like baseball?" Yes.

"Will he play catch with me?" I'm sure.

"Are we getting close?" Not yet.

"How much longer?" About twenty minutes.

"Does he have a big house?" I don't know.

The Sunday before, Lexi and Greg had discussed how to handle the first meeting. They had decided that it would be best to give Kevin a few days to adjust to the idea of his father coming into his life. According to their plan, Lexi waited until the following Thursday evening to tell Kevin that his father had come home from the army and was living in Massachusetts. She explained to him that his father had been injured and it had taken him a long time to get well, but he was better now, so he had come back. When Kevin questioned him about the injuries, she was honest with him. She told him that he had lost his leg in an explosion and that he had learned to walk with an artificial leg. He seemed to accept her explanation about his long absence and his injury without question. That had been a relief.

Lexi was glad that she had not told him any sooner because the child was nearly beside himself for the next two days.

As they drove through the small town of Hull, Lexi couldn't help but notice the charm of the little seaside town. The homes were well-kept and there appeared to be a lot of families out and about. When they arrived at Greg's house, she was impressed. It was a two-story cape cod home on the outer edge of a suburban area, not far from the beach. There was a large deck off to the side and Greg was standing on it waiting for them.

She exited the car and waved at him. She then opened the back door for Kevin. To her surprise, he got out slowly and suddenly he seemed nervous.

The two of them walked to the side of the house and up the steps to the deck.

"Good morning," she said to Greg.

"Good morning, Lex" he returned.

Kevin looked at her with a strange look when he said that.

She put her hand on Kevin's head and spoke. "Kevin this is your father."

Kevin looked at Greg and quietly said, "Hi,"

"Hello," Greg answered. "Did you two have a good trip over here?"

"It was long, but I liked the bridge," Kevin said. "Mom said that you build things. What kind of things do you build?"

"Well," Greg said, "I built this deck and the furniture on it."

Kevin's eyes got big. "That must have taken a long time."

Greg laughed. "It took about three weeks in all. Would either of you like something to drink? I have some iced tea and some soda."

Kevin looked at Lexi. "I haven't had any this weekend."

She smiled. "It will be all right." Then looking at Greg, she explained. "I only allow him to have soda on the weekends and then it is limited."

"That's probably wise," he answered. "Kevin would you like to come in and pick out the drink you want?"

The child gave one quick look to his mother for reassurance. She nodded and then said, "You two go ahead. I think I will stay out here and enjoy the sunshine. I would like some tea though."

Kevin's Wish

Lexi sat down on the swing and looked around. Off to the right, she could see that there was a large metal building that was connected to the house by a concrete sidewalk. She supposed that was where he built the furniture When she looked at the houses across the road, she could see a glimpse of the ocean between them. It was a particularly nice day for mid-September in Massachusetts and the neighborhood had a peaceful, friendly feel to it.

Ten minutes later, Greg and Kevin returned. Kevin was carrying a can of Coke and a glass of iced tea, which he handed to his mother. Greg had another coke and a bowl filled with caramel corn.

The three of them sat on the deck and made small talk for a while. Greg asked Kevin about school and his friends. Lexi could tell that he was trying not to press too hard. To her relief, she could also see Kevin begin to relax. He became more talkative with the answer to each question.

Suddenly, Kevin looked up and pointed to the sky. "What is that?" he asked.

Greg and Lexi both looked up to where Kevin was pointing, which over the houses across the road.

Greg smiled. "Someone is flying a kite on the beach," he said.

"Cool," Kevin said. "That is a big kite."

"I was thinking that we could take a walk down the beach," Greg told them. "There is a really good seafood grill not too far from here. They have an outdoor seating area with a nice beach view. They have good hamburgers, if you don't like seafood."

"Is shrimp seafood?" Kevin asked.

Lexi laughed. "Yes, honey. Shrimp is most definitely seafood."

"I love shrimp," Kevin told his father.

"Great," Greg said. "Is that all right with you, Lex?"

Before she could answer, Kevin asked Greg, "Why do you call her Lex?"

Greg looked at him and said, "Well, I guess you could say it is a nickname that I have been calling her for a long time."

Kevin's Wish

"What's a nickname?"

"A nickname is like a special name or a shortened name that you give to people that you know really well," Greg explained.

Kevin thought about that for a moment and then asked a question. "Are you going to give me a nickname?"

Greg and Lexi looked at one another and both of them realized that there was a hidden meaning behind the question.

"I think maybe a good nickname for you would be Kev," Greg said. "What do you think?"

"Yeah, and I will call you Dad instead of Daddy."

Lexi smiled. Life was simple in the world of a five-year old.

The rest of the afternoon went well. The three of them walked down to the beach. They stopped to watch the kite flyers. Kevin was completely fascinated. He talked to Greg about it all the way down the beach.

The dinner was delicious. As Lexi enjoyed her lobster roll, she felt pleased and relieved. It was almost as if she weren't there. The conversation between Greg and Kevin was nearly non-stop. Most of it centered around the possibility of purchasing a kite and flying it the following weekend.

Greg picked up his phone and did some looking. Then he handed the phone to Kevin. "What do you think of that one?"

"That is cool," Kevin said with a tone of absolute delight.

Greg hit some buttons and said "Done. It will be here by Wednesday."

"When can we fly it?" Kevin asked excitedly.

Greg looked at Lexi. "Next weekend?"

She looked back at him, trying to figure a way around the problem that she had just realized. "Next weekend," she began slowly, "there is a charity event at the college, and I am committed to volunteer all day Saturday." She looked at her son and it tore at her heart to see his face fall.

"Oh, that's too bad," Greg said. He looked at Kevin and thought for a moment.

Kevin's Wish

"I could drive up and get you on Saturday morning," he suggested, "but only if it's all right with your mother."

Kevin looked at his mother with a face full of hope. How could she deny him?

"I don't see why not," she said. "Actually, it solves a problem. I wasn't sure what I was going to do with you while I was working at the event anyway."

"Then it's settled," Greg said. "What time do you have to be at the college?"

"Nine o'clock," she told him. "Why don't I take him with me, and you can just pick him up there?"

"Sounds like a plan," he answered.

Chapter Two

On the following Saturday Lexi was at the college early, setting up the registration table where she was assigned to work most of the day. Kevin was going back and forth between the table and the door watching for Greg. He had his backpack strapped to his back and refused to put it down even for a few minutes.

Lexi smiled. The sight of Kevin watching excitedly for his father made her happier than she could have ever imagined that it would. On

Kevin's Wish

Wednesday night, he had absolutely insisted on calling Greg to make sure that the kite had arrived. She texted him first to be sure that he wasn't busy in the shop, and when he texted back that he wasn't, Lexi allowed Kevin to call him. He took the phone to his room and didn't bring it back for thirty minutes. He made no comments when he returned the phone, but he looked very pleased.

Greg came through the door just a couple of minutes before nine. Lexi told herself that the reason that her heart jumped at the sight of him was because she was happy for her son. The warning bells in the back of her head reminded her that she could not afford to be hurt by this man again.

Kevin ran straight to him and gave him a hug. If this surprised Greg, he did not let it show, but just hugged him back. Then he looked over at her and smiled, and the light in his blue eyes that she remembered from years ago seemed to be back.

After Kevin let go of him, Greg walked over to her. "It's going to be a beautiful day," he said. "It's a shame you will be stuck in here all day, while we're out on the beach flying our kite."

"That's all right," she said. "I think that it will be nice for the two of you to spend the day together."

Greg looked down at his son and ruffled the dark brown hair that matched his own. "You are right. It will be."

"This isn't going to be over until after eight," she told him, "and then we will have to do some cleaning up. I think that it will be at least nine before I get out of here."

"You will be tired," Kevin answered. "Why don't you just go on home and come and get him in the morning. I have two extra rooms...or I could bring him back later tonight if you would rather."

Lexi smiled. "It all right, Greg. I trust you with him. As a matter of fact, I packed a few things in his backpack, just in case."

At that point, Kevin literally began to jump up and down. "I get to spend the night with you?"

"It looks that way, buddy," he said. Then he turned to Lexi. "Instructions?"

She thought for a moment, while looking at her son, before she spoke. "Backseat. Seatbelt. Sunscreen. Brush your teeth; for real."

Then she turned to Greg. "He has been known to just wet the toothbrush and think that he could fool me."

Greg laughed. "Thanks for the warning. Are you ready?" he asked, looking at Kevin, who was already three steps toward the door.

"Excuse me," Lexi said. "Aren't you forgetting something?"

"What?" Kevin asked.

"I think you mother would like you to tell her good-bye," Greg answered for her.

"Oh yeah," Kevin said and ran over to give his mother a hug. She hugged and kissed him and then gave him the obligatory mother's warning to be good.

"You won't be offended if I call you a few times, will you?" she asked as they started to move toward the door.

"I fully expect you to," Greg said over his shoulder.

As she watched the two of them walk out to the parking lot, she felt a little lonely and part of her wished that it was the three of them heading off for a day of fun.

"Lexi, Dean Fletcher is looking for you," she heard one of the interns tell her.

"I'm coming," she said giving one last look out the door before turning her attention to her work.

Soon she was so busy helping to organize the event that she didn't have time to worry about her son. It was after four o'clock before she had a chance to call and check on him. Greg reported that had they had both just finished cleaning up and they were going out to eat at a local restaurant. The kite flying had been a resounding success and they had plans to try it again in the morning before the predicted rain moved in. Lexi promised to be there by ten so that she could participate in the morning kite flying.

When she arrived home, around 9:30, she was really glad that she didn't have to make an hour drive to Hull and back that night. She dropped into bed after setting her alarm and was asleep immediately.

The next morning, Lexi woke up to the ringing of her phone. Sitting up in bed, she looked down at her nightstand and realized that Greg was calling her. She grabbed the phone quickly and swallowed hard as she prayed that Kevin was all right.

"Hello? Greg?"

"Hi Lex, Did I wake you up?"

"Yeah, I guess. Is Kevin all right?"

She could feel him smile through the phone. "He's fine. I gather that you haven't left yet?"

"No," she answered, "It's only...oh my, it's nine o'clock. My alarm must not have gone off. I need to get moving."

"No rush," he said, "The rain moved in sooner than expected so we went out earlier, but we are done now. Why don't you just relax? I'll bring him back."

Lexi was actually relieved, but she gave one polite argument. "Are you sure?"

"It's not a problem," he said. "How about I trade the ride back for some breakfast?"

"Deal." she said.

A little over an hour later, the two of them came through the door of her apartment. Lexi was just finishing putting breakfast on the table. She set a plate of bacon next to the stack of pancakes and then poured coffee for her and Greg, all the time listening to Kevin tell her of his adventures.

Greg smiled as he took his first sip of coffee while listening to his son chattering to his mother. He only slowed down when he began to eat his pancakes. A few minutes later, as they finished the meal Kevin began to yawn.

"Mom, can I watch the Incredibles?" he asked. Lexi knew that what he really meant was "I am tired, and I need to fall asleep watching TV".

"Sure, good ahead," she told him. By the time he was on the couch and deeply engrossed in the movie, Lexi and Kevin had cleared the table and were sitting back down with fresh coffee.

"Would you like to work out some sort of schedule for the two of you to spend time together?" Lexi asked.

"That's exactly what I was just hoping," he answered. "I do want to spend time with him, but I don't want to mess up your life."

Lexi looked at him for a moment and tried to analyze what he meant by that. "You are not going to mess up my life," she began. "You are Kevin's father. He needs you in his life. That is important to me."

"I guess since we are still married, I am his father in every sense of the word."

Lexi nodded and answered the unspoken question. "Your name is on his birth certificate."

He thought for a moment and then asked her a question. "You're not worried that I am going to try to take him away from you, are you? Please believe me when I say that I would never think about doing that."

Lexi slowly shook her head. "I'm not concerned about that." After a moment of thought she continued. "Are you over the shock of finding out that we are married?"

Greg looked down and ran his hands through his hair. "What I really can't get over is that you didn't do anything about it. I didn't know about Kevin, but the past few years I have thought that by now that you would have found somebody else."

"After I talked to an online attorney, I just decided that I didn't want to pursue it. We are

Kevin's parents. The thought of taking action to divorce his father just seemed wrong."

"The idea of finding someone else didn't appeal to you?" he asked.

She shook her head. "I am a married woman. How would that look to Kevin? He thought that you were just away working." They were both quiet for a moment. "I always assumed if you wanted out, you would find me. Of course, I didn't know about your memory lapse."

Kevin stared at her intently. "What if I hadn't lost my memory and I had come to you to ask for a divorce? What would you have done?"

Lexi sighed and gathered her emotions. She prepared herself for the possibility of what he might be about to tell her.

"I would have agreed to it," she said. Then she took another breath. "I won't stand in your way now either. If you want out to be with someone else or for whatever reason, we can work something out."

Greg looked at her strangely. "There is no one else," he said. "The night of the wedding I wanted to talk to you, because I wanted to know if we really did get married. I understand what you mean about feeling conflicted about divorcing the other parent of your child. I guess it makes things simpler if we stay married for the time being, because it gives me parental privileges when you are not with me."

Lexi nodded, but didn't comment.

"I will say the same to you," he continued.

"What?" she asked.

"If you decide that you want out, I won't stand in your way either."

His words gave her an empty feeling in the pit of her stomach, but she didn't comment one way or the other. Then she watched him reach into his jacket pocket and pull out an envelope, which he handed to her.

Taking it, she looked inside. There were several bills in it. She took them out and counted them. It amounted to five hundred dollars. Her eyes grew wide as she looked at him.

"I am not trying to imply that you don't have enough money to take care him," he said, "but he is my responsibility too. Take the money please. If there isn't anything he needs right now, save if it for later. I want to do my share."

She smiled. "Thank you."

"Now let's talk about a schedule," he said. "Any thoughts?"

"I know that he is going to want to see you every weekend," she told him. "Is that too much for you?"

"Absolutely not," he said. "What if he stays here with you on Friday nights and Saturday mornings, and I will come to get him on Saturday afternoons, and he can stay with me for the night. Then you can come and get him on Sunday afternoons?"

A strange almost sad feeling went through her. It felt as if they were separating and working out a visitation schedule. "That will be fine, but if things come up like birthday parties or school events, we can always adjust."

"Sure, no problem," he told her. "I was also thinking about maybe driving up on Wednesday evenings and having dinner with him?"

"That would be nice," she answered.

Kevin's Wish

"If he wants to call me in the evenings, that's fine," he told her. "I am already starting to get Christmas orders in, but I just can't seem to work much past seven."

"Your leg?" she asked.

He nodded. "Sometimes it's over exertion and I have to get off the artificial leg and sometimes it's my good leg that gets tired. Once in a while when my leg is sore, I get a phantom pain in my missing foot. That's always strange."

Lexi felt sad looking at him. Her face must have given away her thoughts, because he smiled and said. "It can be tough, but it could be a lot worse. When I was in therapy, one of the therapists gave me a good kick in the ass. I was bitching about the pain and she said, 'Look around! There are guys here missing two legs and even a few missing both arms and legs and some in wheelchairs that will never walk again. Then there are those who are so brain damaged that they can't even tell you their names, and guess what? They are all working harder than you! So get off your ass and start getting better!' That moment was a game changer for me. From then on, I didn't look back. Anytime I have pain I think about some of those other guys and thank God that I wasn't one of them."

Lexi didn't know how to respond to that, but he spared her from having to. "I really need to start back. I have some things that I need to get done." He then walked over to the living room area and stared down at the couch. Lexi followed him and saw that Kevin was stretched out and sound asleep.

"I guess you wore him out," she said.

"I think so," he answered. As he walked to the door, he said, "Tell him I said good-bye and I'll see him Wednesday."

"I will," she told him. "Thanks again for bringing him back."

"Thank you for breakfast," he said. Then he stared at her for a moment, before saying, "Good-bye, Lex."

She smiled and said, "Good-bye Greg."

After she closed the door behind him, she felt the same sadness that she did when the two of them had left the day before. She did her best to shake it off before she locked the door and began to wash the breakfast dishes.

Kevin's Wish

On Wednesday afternoon while Lexi was still at work, her cell phone began to ring. She looked down and saw that it was her sister, Angie. She smiled, thinking she must be back from her trip to San Francisco. Her husband, Gary, had a job that involved a great deal of traveling. Since they had no children, Angie often traveled with him. This particular event lasted four days and then they had left on an extended cruise to Canada and Alaska. Lexi had not talked to her since she had left. She had decided that it would be easier to explain the recent changes in her life to her sister once she had returned.

"Hi, Ange, how was the trip?"

"It was great, thanks. We had a wonderful time. I can't wait to show you and Kevin the pictures. I was hoping you would think about coming to Georgia for Thanksgiving."

"Well, I would like to, but this does tie in with some news that I have to tell you," Lexi said, and then she proceeded to tell her everything that had happened in the last few weeks.

When she finished, Angie was quiet, and Lexi assumed that she was trying to process all of the information that she had just been given.

"Ange?" Lexi finally asked as she thought that she heard her sister sniffling.

"I just..."

"Do you think I made a mistake in letting Greg into Kevin's life?"

"No!" Angie answered adamantly. "You know that I was always Greg's biggest fan. I adored him and I thought that you gave up on him too soon. I am just amazed that according to what you just told me, that the transition was so smooth. Kevin is completely attached to his father?"

"Completely," she said, "and vice versa. I think that the fact that Kevin is still very young helps. At his age, he is still very innocent and accepting."

"Do you think that Greg is in this for the long haul?" Angie asked. "There is no chance that Kevin is just a novelty for now, is there?"

Lexi was a little surprised at her question. "No, I don't think so," she answered. "Every time I see him, he seems more and more like the old Greg. I think spending time with Kevin is really good for him."

"Hmm," Angie said. "That's interesting. What about the two of you? You are married. Are you planning to stay that way?"

"We have discussed that situation," Lexi told her. "We decided that it is in Kevin's best interest for us to stay married for the time being."

"So, you are back together again, romantically?"

There was a pause before Lexi answered her sister. "No, we're not. It's just that we are all adjusting to our new situation, and we don't want to complicate things any more than they already are. We did both agree that if the other wanted out, we would not stand in each other's way."

"I take that to mean that he doesn't have a girlfriend or significant other of any kind?"

"No, I asked him, and he said that he didn't."

"Hmm," Angie responded. "Lexi?"

"What?"

"Are you still in love with him?"

When she didn't respond, Angie continued. "This is me you are talking to. Be honest."

Lexi tried very hard to control her emotions. "I'm trying very hard not to be," she answered.

"Why?"

"Because I'm scared," she said.

There was a silence before Angie answered. "I guess I can understand that. It's a slippery slope, isn't it?"

"Yes, it is. Thanks for understanding. I can only hope that Mom will be this understanding."

Angie gave a small laugh. "Would you like me to break the news to her?"

"Would you, please?" she answered with a sigh of relief. "I have been seriously avoiding that conversation."

"I will break the news, but you know that you will hear from her."

"I know," Lexi said.

"I guess the problem with Thanksgiving is that it would be the first holiday that Kevin and Greg would be able to share?"

"Right."

"Lexi, Greg would be more than welcome to join us," Angie told her.

"That's very considerate of you," Lexi said. "I'll have to think about that and of course discuss it with Greg. It is still only September, though."

"I know," Angie answered, "but if you are going to fly you will need to think about getting tickets."

"That is true," Lexi told her. "Let's just see how it works out."

"Oh, my goodness," Angie laughed. "Mom is calling me right now. I guess I'll go ahead and break this news to her. Goodbye."

"Bye,"

Ten minutes after she finished talking to her sister, Greg texted her that he had just pulled into the parking lot. She texted him back and gave him the directions to the dean's office.

It wasn't long before Greg was standing in front of her desk. She was on the phone taking a message when he came in, but she couldn't help but notice how nice he looked in his jeans, polo shirt and jacket. Once again, she felt the sense of the old Greg standing there. She motioned him to a chair, and he sat down and waited.

"Hi," she said, after she finished, then she looked at her cell phone. "I haven't gotten the text from the after-school center that he has gotten off the bus yet, but it is a little early. I have something I want to talk to you about anyway.

"What's that?" he asked, looking almost worried.

She then told him about the conversation she just had had with her sister concerning Thanksgiving.

She finished by telling him that it wasn't something that had to be decided immediately, but they could both give it some thought.

"If you want to take Kevin to Georgia for Thanksgiving I would understand," Greg told her.

"She wanted me to invite you to come too," she said. "Angie has always liked you and I think she might be looking forward to seeing you."

He smiled. "I always liked her too," he said. "Have you talked to your mother about me yet?"

"Angie is talking to her right now about our situation."

"You mean that you haven't told your mother about me being back in your life?"

Lexi shook her head.

He smiled. "Lex, you always did melt into a puddle of goo around your mother."

"Guilty," she said. "Anyway, we can table the Thanksgiving situation until later, unless you already have other plans. Something tells me though, that you don't spend much time with your sister?" she asked.

Greg stared at her for a moment and then said, "I haven't spoken with Ellen in four years."

"That's very unfortunate," Lexi told him.

Greg did not comment any further, and her phone beeped, and she glanced at it and saw that Kevin had arrived from school. "I'll walk you over to the center," she said. "You can show your identification and fill out some paperwork so that you will be able to pick him up without me. Then I have to work another hour."

"Sounds good," he said.

Just before they reached the door of the center, Lexi's phone rang again. It was her mother. She held it up for Greg to see the name and then answered it.

"Hi, Mom. I'm at work and I'm kind of busy at the moment. Can I call you back in about an hour?"

She heard her mother sigh. "All right, but don't forget."

"I won't. Talk to you later. Bye."

She gave Greg a dirty look, because she swore that she heard him say, "Chicken," under his breath.

As Lexi entered her apartment after work, she set her purse down on the kitchen counter and realized that she couldn't avoid it any longer. She had to call her mother. If she didn't, she knew that her mother would just call her and then she would be irritated.

After pulling her phone out of her purse, she walked over to the couch and sat down and began to dial.

"Hello."

"Hi, Mom."

"Lexi, do you have time to talk to me now?"

"Yes, Mom. I am now home alone so I have all the time in the world." Then she immediately regretted saying that she was home alone.

"Where is Kevin?"

"Greg took him out to dinner."

"That's nice. I thought Angie said that he lives an hour away."

"Yes, he lives in Hull, but he drove up here to see Kevin."

"Hmm. Lexi, why didn't you tell me?"

"I was planning to tell you, Mom. I didn't tell Angie until today."

"She was out of town. I wasn't. I am a little hurt. This was big news. Why didn't you want to share it with me?"

"I am sorry. I was going to call you. It just that it has been an adjustment and...I didn't know how you were going to feel about it. Greg hasn't been very high on your list in the last few years."

"You're right about that, but Angie did explain that you learned some things that have shed some new light on the situation."

"To be honest, I was afraid that you would say something like, 'Do you really believe that?'. In case you are wondering about that; yes, I do believe him. We discussed our marriage and his memory loss before I told him about Kevin. When I told him that he had a five-year-old son, tears actually came to his eyes. I believe he is genuine about wanting to be a major role in his son's life, and before you ask, he has already given me money and absolutely insisted that I take it."

"Lexi, I guess I understand why you might think that way, but what you didn't guess correctly was that I am happy for Kevin. I know how badly he was searching for a father figure in his life. I pray that this works out for all of you. Angie said that you plan to stay married?"

Lexi thought for a moment about how to answer the question. "I think that the best way to put it is that we decided not to rush into any impulsive decisions right away."

Kevin's Wish

She could feel her mother contemplating her words before she answered. "That seems wise."

"Mom, Greg is trying to call me. I better take the call since Kevin is with him. I'll call you in a few days."

"All right, honey. Good-bye."

"Bye."

"Hi Greg. Is everything all right?"

It turned out to be Kevin. "Hi Mom. We need to come home and change my clothes."

"Why?"

"We went to Lowe's and I kind of got some mulch all over me."

"How did you do that?"

"Dad was loading bags onto his truck and I was trying to help him, and a bag broke all over me. Are you home so that we can get in?"

Lexi stifled a laugh. "Yes, honey. I am home."

"Ok, we'll be right there."

Lexi shook her head and headed for the bedroom. She pulled some clean clothes out of his dresser and laid them on the bed. Then she got a clothes basket out of the closet to drop his smelly clothes in. It looked like her evening was now planned. She was going to spend it at the laundry.

A few minutes later, she heard them coming through the door. She looked at her son and had to laugh.

"Come on," she told him. She ushered him into the bathroom and supervised a quick shower. Within twenty minutes she presented Greg with his son, now freshly cleaned and clothed. She was carrying the laundry basket with his smelly clothes in a bag and a few other items that needed washed.

"Are you going to the laundry, Mom?" Kevin asked.

"I think I have to," she said with a smile. "Thank you very much."

Greg looked at her with a concerned face. "I'm sorry, Lex. I let him get dirty and now your evening is ruined."

Kevin's Wish

She laughed. "Don't worry about it. Do you know how many times that he has done things like that to me?"

"You don't have a washer and dryer in the apartment?" he asked.

"No," she said. "There is one on the second floor. I'll just take a book and get some reading done. It won't take long."

He seemed to think for a moment before he spoke. "Why don't you come to dinner with us? We are going to Red Lobster."

Lexi frowned. "That's not fair. You know how I love that place, but If I don't do these tonight, they will really smell by morning."

Looking at Greg, she could see that his wheels were still turning. He walked over to the basket and picked the bag up out of it. "I dirtied them. I'll wash them. I will throw them into my washer to soak when I get home, and I can finish them tomorrow. That way you won't have to send extra clothes on Saturday, and you can come to dinner with us tonight. What do you think Kev?"

"Yeah, Mommy. Come with us."

She looked at her son. She could never resist "Mommy" and he knew it.

An hour later, she was enjoying coconut shrimp, and she and Greg were both laughing at their son's antics as he was telling them all about his kindergarten world. It felt almost as if they were a family.

Chapter Three

The next six weeks passed peacefully and quietly. The plan for Greg and Kevin to spend time together worked out very well. Sometimes when Kevin was gone, Lexi enjoyed her time alone and other times she felt somewhat lonely. She often caught herself wondering what they were doing and if they were having fun. It wasn't that she resented the time that the two of them were spending together. It was, she finally admitted to herself, that she wished she were a part of it.

During the second week of October, Lexi went for a job interview at one of the local newspaper offices. The job involved being a researcher and a general assistant to two of the editors. There was one drawback, which was that there were no benefits involved. Fortunately, two weeks earlier Greg had had Kevin placed on his military insurance. Since they were married, he had told her that he could put her on the same family plan. She hadn't taken him up on that offer, but it was still a possibility she could consider. The wages offered were the most attractive part of the job, and between that possibility and the money Greg had promised to give her on a monthly basis, Lexi began to consider moving to a larger apartment. The interview went very well, and Lexi left feeling very confident that she was going to be offered the position.

Ten days later, Lexi was in the kitchen, washing the dinner dishes, when Kevin came in and asked her if he could use the phone to call his father. She nodded without comment and he took the phone off the table and went to his room.

Fifteen minutes later, he came back and handed the phone to her.

"Dad wants to talk to you," he said.

A little surprised, she took the phone from him and watched him leave the room.

"Hello,"

"Hi, Lex. What's going on?"

"Not much. Why do you ask?"

"Kevin said that you seemed upset about something," he said. "I just wanted to make sure that you were all right."

Lexi caught her breath. In the midst of her concerns over the troublesome news that she had just received, she had forgotten how perceptive her son was.

"I've just had a very bad week," she told him.

"Is this about the job?" he asked.

"Partly," she answered.

"Did they offer it to you?"

"The woman from the newspaper called me yesterday morning," she began. "She said that

that the owners of the paper had rethought the situation and eliminated the position that I interviewed for and replaced it with three part time jobs which would be labeled as stay at home positions. The hourly wage would be the same, but there would be less hours. She offered me one of the positions, and I told her I would think about it. I took today off work to do some number crunching and give the situation some serious thought, and I came to the conclusion that it just might work. While I wouldn't be able to move right now, working from home would be an advantage, because Kevin wouldn't have to go to an afterschool program. It would save money and he could come straight home."

"So, you are going to take the job?"

"That was my plan, right up until I opened my email this afternoon."

"I have a feeling that it was not good news?"

She sighed. "My rent is going up, effective the first of next month."

"Oh no," he said. "A lot?"

She sighed and told him what she would be paying.

"Whoa," he said. "That is a lot of money for a two-bedroom apartment in that part of town."

"It's more than you think," she told him. "This is only a one bedroom."

"What?" he said sounding surprised.

"Kevin sleeps in the bedroom," she said, "and I sleep on the pullout couch."

"I had no idea," he said.

"It's not that big of a deal," she said. "I don't mind sleeping on the pullout. I can sleep about anywhere."

She could feel him smile through the phone. "I remember," he said.

"Anyway, I have some decisions to make. Do I stay at the college? The rumors are flying fast and furious about the campus closing. Some of the stories going around are that it won't even be open in January." She sighed. "Sometimes...I just get tired...of ...being a grownup." Then she realized that her voice was cracking.

"Lex, listen to me. I'm not going to stand by and let anything happen to either one of you. Please let me help you figure this out."

She pulled a paper towel off the roll and wiped her eyes. "Are you still there?" he asked.

She smiled a little. "I'm still here," she said. "Thank you. It's nice to not feel so alone."

"Yes, it is," he told her. "I have an idea. When I come to get Kev tomorrow, why don't you come too? I have a third bedroom upstairs that you would be welcome to stay in. We'll make it a fun day for the three of us. Then after Kevin goes to sleep, you and I can have a long talk and maybe I can help you figure some of this out. What do you think? Please? I hate to leave you alone when you are upset."

She smiled at the thought of him being concerned about her, ignoring the distant warning bells going off somewhere in the back of her mind. "I think I would like that. Thank you, Greg."

"All right, I'll see you tomorrow then. Good night, Lex."

"Good night."

Kevin's Wish

Greg kept good on his promise. The three of them did have an enjoyable day together. It was a warm fall day and they went to the beach and Kevin showed off his newly acquired kite flying skills. Just as they were starting to walk back toward the house, they spotted a pod of dolphins.

They stopped to watch the beautiful creatures for a few minutes.

"Last week we saw a whale, didn't we Dad?"

Greg grinned down at his son. "We saw what I think might have been a whale way off in the distance, but I couldn't be sure without binoculars."

"Next spring, we are going to a place where we can see them better. What is it called again Dad?"

"Race Point," Greg told him.

Lexi smiled. "At Provincetown?"

"Have you been there, Mom?"

She nodded. "When I was a little girl, your grandfather used to take my sister and me there to watch for whales."

"Did you see any?" Kevin wanted to know.

"Yes, we saw quite a few over the years," she said.

"Cool," he said. "I can't wait."

Greg and Lexi exchanged a smile that parents often do when they see joy on the face of their child.

Later the three of them went to a local restaurant and enjoyed a delicious meal. When they were finished, Greg drove them around the town of Hull, pointing out various places of interest. When they passed the elementary school, Kevin asked, "Is that where Billy goes to school?"

Greg glanced at the building. "I believe it is," he answered. Then he looked over at Lexi. "Billy is a little boy that lives down the street from me. His father is a buddy of mine. He has brought Billy over to play a few times and I have taken him down there. He and Kevin are about the same age."

"He's in kindergarten too," Kevin added.

"I see," Lexi answered. That's nice for him to have a friend in your neighborhood."

"Yes, it is," Greg answered somewhat thoughtfully.

Later that night when Kevin was in bed asleep, Greg and Lexi sat at his kitchen table and began discussing her current situation.

"You haven't arrived at any decisions since we talked last night, have you?" Greg asked her.

"If I had to make a decision right now, I would probably turn the job down and just stay where I am, while I continue to look for another job," she told him. "With your support money, I can get by for the time being."

He nodded. "I could give you more," he said. Then he was quiet for a moment before he continued.

"Everything else aside, the newspaper job appealed to you, didn't it?"

She looked over at him. Even after all this time, he knew her well. It was still like he could read her mind, so she didn't respond, but only nodded.

"I have been thinking about this and I have a couple of scenarios that I would like to suggest," he said.

Lexi was a little surprised and curious. "I'm listening," she said.

"I have a couple of issues going on in my life right now too, and I think we could help each other out."

Lexi didn't respond, but just waited for him to continue.

"The first is about Kevin. It is almost amazing how quickly I have grown to love that boy. He has become the center of my world. Do you know what I mean?"

A slow smile spread across Lexi's face, and she nodded at him. "And you have become a large part of his life. I knew he needed a father, but I had no idea how much. You are so good for him."

"I think so too," he told her. "You aren't intimidated by the time we spend together, are you?"

"Absolutely not," she said, "so what is the issue you are having with him?"

Greg looked her straight in the eye. "I really want to see more of him," he said. "I have been tossing this around even before we talked about your problem. I've even considered the possibility of moving to Brookline, but after thinking about your situation, I have come up with another idea."

"What is that?" she asked.

"What if you were to move here to Hull? You could take the part time job and work at home and we could both have more time with Kevin. Then if you were willing, you could help me with a problem that I have."

"Which is?"

"I need some help with my business," he told her. "I have a website, but I only take orders by phone at this point. I am overloaded with orders to be filled before Christmas, but I think I can handle it. I have hired a few kids from the vocational school to come in and help me with cutting wood, painting and staining, which is really going to help. I just can't keep stopping to answer the phone to tell people that their order is on schedule and to tell others that I can't take any more Christmas orders. I need help keeping my paperwork organized too."

"So, you need a part time secretary?"

"Exactly," he said. "I realize that Kevin would have to change schools, and maybe asking both of you to uproot your lives is too much. If you don't want to do this, I will understand. We can work something else out for Kevin and I to spend more time together."

Lexi looked at him for a moment. "I would consider moving here to Hull. There is nothing for me in Brookline. I only moved there for the job, which I think will be gone soon. I don't even have any family left in Massachusetts anymore. There is just one thing that concerns me."

"What?"

"I would still have the same problem," she said. "I wouldn't make enough money to pay rent for a decent place for Kevin and me to live in."

"I have an idea about that too," he said. "You could live here. Since my room is downstairs, the two of you could have the whole upstairs."

Lexi tried to keep her mouth from dropping open. This was not what she was expecting him to say. She had totally expected him to offer to pay rent for her on an apartment and she was trying to consider how she would feel about accepting that kind of help from him. This, however, came clear out of left field.

"It seems to be a simple solution, but if it makes you uncomfortable, I understand," he said.

After a minute, she responded. "I see how it makes sense," she told him, "but let's look at the big picture. Are we talking about a permanent arrangement or a temporary one? Because Kevin would love the whole idea and then it would be hard to go backward and go back to having separate homes again. He would be crushed."

"You're right," he said. "I hadn't thought about it that way."

They were both quiet for a few minutes. Eventually Greg broke the silence. "Last week he asked me if we were married or divorced."

"Really?"

"Apparently some of the kids at school were talking about the status of their parents and he wasn't sure about to tell his friends about his parents."

"What did you say to him?"

Greg sighed. "I told him that we are married, but we had been living apart because I because I had been hurt. Then I told him that we had jobs in separate towns."

"Let me guess that next he asked if we were ever going to live in the same town?"

"No," Greg said, "surprisingly he didn't, but I could tell that he was thinking about that."

There was another moment of silence. Then Lexi looked up at him. "We have some decisions to make about the future, don't we?"

"What do you want to do?" he asked her. "Do you want a divorce or an annulment?"

Lexi could not bring herself to answer the question. She didn't even want to think about divorcing him, but she just couldn't bring herself to admit to him that she was still in love with him. The fear of rejection was just too great. She felt caught between a rock and a hard place.

"I don't know what I want," she told him. "I am trying to think about Kevin and what is best for him, but I'm just not sure. What about you? How do you feel about it?"

He sighed. "I'm not sure what's best for him either." He was quiet for a moment. "I have a suggestion. Why don't the two of you come and stay here through the holidays? We will make it clear to Kevin that this is a visit and that after

Christmas we will make more permanent arrangements. Then, after the first of the year, you and I will make some decisions. You would be welcome to stay if you want, but if you decide that you want your own place than I will help you in any way that I can."

The suggestion of moving in here sent a surge of warmth through her. She knew that eventually she might face some heartache over this decision but sitting here alone with him in his kitchen brought a sense of happiness to her that she just couldn't resist.

"All right," she told him. "That sounds like a plan. There is one thing that I think we should agree to though."

"What is that?"

"No matter what decisions that we make or what the future brings, we will raise Kevin together as his parents, equally."

At her words, Greg's face lit up with happiness. "Absolutely," he answered. "We will raise our son together."

The transition was simple and smooth. The following weekend, Lexi and Kevin moved into the upstairs part of Greg's house. She had no regrets about leaving Brookline or her apartment, however she did feel somewhat sad about leaving Paul and the college. When she gave him her notice, he was completely understanding. He then went on to tell her in confidence that the rumors circulating were mostly true. The college would be open only on a limited basis after the first of the year and completely closed by the spring quarter. He went on to tell her that he thought that she had made a good decision in moving her son closer to his father.

By Sunday evening, the two of them were settled in and Greg took some time to go through his business records with Lexi. It seemed pretty simple and she was sure that she could help him. She wasn't starting her new job for a couple of weeks, which was a good thing because it allowed her some time to get organized. The two of them worked out a schedule and discussed some rules and guidelines for Kevin.

The next morning, Greg and Lexi registered Kevin for school together. If the child was nervous or scared, he did not show it at all. Fortunately, he was placed in the same classroom as his friend Billy, so the two of them felt good about the situation. Lexi liked the school. It had a much friendlier feel than his school in Brookline. His new teacher was young and seemed to have a pleasant personality.

The next morning Lexi took Kevin outside to wait for the bus. The bus stop was at the end of the road and since their house was on the corner, the stop was just off the end of their driveway. Kevin was excited to return to school since he had had a wonderful first day. While they were waiting, several other parents and children walked up to wait for the bus. They all smiled a greeting at Lexi. Just before the bus was scheduled to arrive, Kevin got excited and called out to his friend.

"Billy!"

Lexi turned around and saw a small brown-haired boy running toward Kevin. He was followed by a woman who must have been his mother. She was a petite brunette with hair that fell below her shoulders. Lexi had the impression that she had left the house hurriedly. She was wearing thin sweatpants and a t-shirt, with a long sweater that she had wrapped tightly around herself. It had turned sharply colder overnight and apparently; she had not gotten that bulletin.

When she caught up with her son, she looked at Lexi and smiled. "Hi," she said. "You must be Kevin's mother?"

Lexi smiled back. "Yes, I'm Lexi Carter. Nice to meet you." She held out her hand.

"I'm Kami Michaels. Welcome to the neighborhood. Billy has been very excited about Kevin being in his class."

Lexi smiled. "Kevin has been going on and on about Billy too." At that point their conversation ended because the bus pulled up to the stop.

After the children were securely on the bus, the parents all turned and began to disperse to their various homes. Lexi smiled at Kami and said, "It was nice to meet you."

"It was nice to meet you too," Kami said as she pulled her sweater even tighter. "Oh my, it's cold."

On a sudden impulse, Lexi spoke up. "Would you like to come in and have a cup of coffee?"

Kami looked up at her and seemed to be considering the offer. Then she suddenly said, "Yes, I think I would like that."

As they drank their coffee, the two women made small talk; at first it was mostly about their sons and the up-coming Christmas season. Then Lexi learned that Kami worked part time at a local insurance company and that her husband, Bill, was an accountant. Kami then asked her about her new job and Lexi realized that Greg must have discussed their situation to some extent with his neighbors. She then began to wonder just how much Kami and her husband did know about their history as husband and wife.

Just as they were finishing their coffee and Kami had agreed to *"just one more cup"*, Greg walked into the kitchen from the shop.

When he saw the two of them sitting at the table, he smiled.

"Hi, Kami," he said in a familiar way.

"Hey, Greg," she responded.

Greg looked at Lexi and spoke. "I have to go get some supplies for the shop. Do you need anything from the store or anywhere?"

"I don't think so," she told him, "but thanks for asking."

"All right then," he said. "I'll be back in an hour or so."

"Ok," she answered.

The two women were quiet for a moment after he left. Kami finally spoke up and answered the question that was going through Lexi's mind.

"In case you were wondering, Greg did explain to us why you and Kevin have not been in his life until recently."

"You mean that he didn't know of Kevin's existence?"

"Yes, and that he had some sort of amnesia and didn't remember that you two had gotten married. He also told us about pushing you away and how his sister didn't treat you very well when you tried to contact him after Kevin was born. He made it very clear that he didn't blame you in any way for the lost years."

Lexi stared at her new friend. The words that she had just said brought a smile to her face. She silently thanked Greg for putting her in a good light to his friends.

"It is an unusual situation," she said, "and Greg has been more gracious and generous than a lot of men might have been."

"Bill and I have always liked Greg," Kami answered, "but since the two of you have come into his life, he has been a whole new person. He seems to be so happy."

"Kevin and he bonded immediately," Lexi said. "I'm just along by default."

Kami got a strange look on her face. "Are you sure about that?" she asked.

Before Lexi could answer, Kami's cell phone rang. She answered it and had a brief conversation. After she hung up, she sighed. "That was my Aunt Gracie. She lives in an apartment across town, and she doesn't drive. Somehow, I have become her caretaker. She needs some things from the store. I guess I better get moving, so I can get back and take care of my day off chores before Billy gets home. I have really enjoyed this though. Thanks for the coffee."

"Thank you for the company," Lexi answered.

Lexi watched Kami head down the street with her sweater pulled tightly around her. She was happy to have found a new friend, but she was still trying to figure out what she had meant by the words, *"Are you sure about that?"*.

The following Saturday night was Halloween. Kevin and Billy decided that they wanted to be ghosts. Lexi decided that was an easy fix. She went to Walmart and bought some light blue sheets and cut them down to the boy's sizes. She then made some belts from the leftover material and drew some scary faces on them. The boys seemed elated with their costumes.

Since Lexi had taken Kevin trick or treating the last couple of years, she stayed back to hand out candy while Greg and Bill took the boys from house to house in the neighborhood.

When the time was up the group all met at the Michaels' house. They ate Kami's homemade vegetable soup and then while the boys watched movies in the living room, their parents sat in the kitchen and played cards.

Lexi found Bill Michaels to be a likeable person. She could see how he and Greg were good friends. He was one of those people with a dry sense of humor. He could be telling a story and completely pull you in and then you realize that he is making every bit of it up.

The four of them had an enjoyable evening. Around ten thirty, Greg and Lexi bundled Kevin up and the three of them walked the short distance back to their house. Kevin was exhausted and went immediately to bed. After he was settled Lexi went downstairs and was going through the freezer looking for some meat to lay out for the next day.

"That was fun, wasn't it?" Greg asked, walking into the kitchen from his room.

She looked up. "Yes, it was. I like both Bill and Kami. They are nice people." She pulled a roast out and set it on the counter. "Kami certainly wants one of those sleigh beds that you make."

Greg smiled. "She is getting one for Christmas. It is a secret. Don't tell."

Now Lexi smiled. "Really? That's awesome. I won't say a word. I wouldn't want to spoil a surprise like that."

She thought for a moment. "I was wondering about something. They only have one child. Is there a reason?"

"Yeah," Greg answered. "Actually, Billy is adopted. He is Bill's nephew. His sister gave birth to him and she has a lot of issues of some sort. Anyway, they adopted him shortly after he was born, and the sister took off to California or somewhere. Kami had some sort of problem at a young age and I don't think she can have any children of her own."

"Oh, that's sad," Kami said. "I'm glad you told me that. I would hate to have said something awkward."

"Bill has told me about it, but I have never heard Kami mention it," Greg told her.

There was a moment of silence and then Greg changed the subject. "I was thinking about finding a movie on TV. Do you want to watch with me?"

Lexi smiled to herself, thinking that sounded just like old times. "I'll make the popcorn," she told him.

"I'll find the movie," he said. "Something adventurous?"

"Oh yeah," she answered.

Ten minutes later, the two of them were sitting closely together on the couch, sharing a bowl of popcorn. Lexi felt happier than she had in a long time. Years ago, she and Greg used to love watching movies at night, while munching on popcorn.

When the bowl was empty, Greg set it on the far end of the table and then propped his legs on the coffee table. He made no effort to distance himself from her, so she didn't either. She put her own legs up and relaxed enjoying the closeness of him.

Sometime later, Lexi opened her eyes and realized that she was stretched out on the couch and she was covered up with a blanket. She sat up and looked around. Looking at the DVR clock, she saw that it was three fifteen. Greg must have turned the TV off and then covered her up before he went to bed. She smiled as she thought of the evening she had spent. For just a few moments, she dared to think that things might just work out with Greg. She allowed herself that few moments of pleasure before she put her wall of protection back up. Then she went upstairs to her room alone.

Chapter Four

With Halloween over, November moved in and brought cooler fall weather with a hint of winter in the air.

The new job turned out to be everything that Lexi hoped that would it be. The first week in November, she went to Brookline for two days of orientation and training. The work was interesting, and she was able to manage doing her work and help Greg keep organized while keeping up with Kevin's needs and the household chores.

Lexi's friendship with Kami grew. A couple of mornings a week, the two of them enjoyed coffee after putting their sons on the bus,

About two weeks into the month, Lexi and Kami went shopping at a flea market near Boston. It was the first time since Kevin was born that Lexi had enjoyed a day with a girlfriend. Greg was busy in the shop, but he encouraged them to go and not worry about the boys. He promised to get both of them off the bus and keep them busy sanding wood and pounding small nails into scrap wood.

The two women enjoyed their day. After leaving the flea market they went to a mall and got a start on some Christmas shopping. Both boys were wanting bicycles for Christmas and they found a sale. After some quick calls to Bill and Greg they purchased the bicycles and stowed them in the back of Kami's SUV. Kami explained that there was a retired couple that lived next door to them who were always happy to hide Christmas presents for them. She was sure that they would not minding keeping Kevin's gifts under wraps also.

With Thanksgiving approaching, Lexi knew that she had to make a decision about her sister's invitation. The idea of seeing her sister over the holiday was appealing, but there was a part of her that would like to stay home and cook a traditional meal for Greg and Kevin.

She brought up the subject to Greg and he told her that he didn't feel that he could take the time away from his work. His orders were all scheduled to be finished and shipped by the tenth of December. He told her that if she wanted to fly to Atlanta with Kevin, he didn't have a problem with that.

One evening a few weeks before the holiday, Lexi pulled out her laptop and began to research available flights. She sighed as she realized that she had waited too long. The only flights left were outrageously expensive.

She was sitting on the couch in the living room with the computer closed on her lap thinking about the situation, when Greg walked in.

"Your potatoes were about to boil over," he said. "I turned them down."

She looked up. "Oh thanks. I forgot about them."

"All wrapped up in your work?" he asked as he sat down in the recliner and opened a diet coke.

"No," she answered. "I was checking flights to Atlanta."

"Did you find any?" he asked taking a swig of his coke.

"Oh yeah," she told him, "for a small fortune. I'm not doing that. Then I googled the drive. It's about sixteen hours. That's two days each way. I'm not doing that either. So, I guess we will have our turkey here."

"Are you sure?" he asked. "I would not be comfortable with the two of you driving alone, but I could help with the tickets."

Lexi looked at Greg. Not for the first time, she wondered about his financial situation. He seemed very comfortable. She knew that he was making a nice profit from his furniture business and he received a small salary from teaching classes at the vocational school. She had worked that much out from helping him with his paperwork. He could possibly be receiving some veteran's benefit, she supposed, but she just had the feeling that there was something that she was missing.

"Thank you," she answered, "but not only are the tickets expensive, but the only flights left have odd hours and difficult connections. I don't want to fly to Dallas with a five-year-old in order to get to Atlanta."

"I don't blame you," he said. "Then we will have Thanksgiving here? You didn't want to go to the Fletcher's or anything?"

"No," she answered. "I think a quiet dinner here will be nice. I asked Kami what they are doing, and she said they are taking Aunt Gracie to her parents' house in New Bedford."

"You haven't talked to Angie yet?"

"No, I thought I would call her after dinner," Lexi told him. "Speaking of which, I better check on my meatloaf."

"Lex?"

"What?"

"When I asked you to move in here, I didn't mean for you to become chief cook and bottle washer. It's nice, but I feel bad that you seem to be doing more than your share."

She smiled. "I enjoy it. It's nice to be out of that small apartment and have room to spread out. Cooking is fun in a nice sized kitchen. I know how busy you are right now. Besides, you are paying more than your share of the bills."

He was thoughtful for a moment before he spoke. "Have you thought anymore about what you want to do after the holidays?"

"I haven't come to any decisions, if that's what you mean," she told him. "I am just enjoying being here for now."

He smiled. "I'm glad."

She smiled back. "Dinner will be ready soon. Kevin is awfully quiet up in his room. Would you mind going up and checking on him?"

"I will take care of that," he answered as he stood and started for the stairs.

Lexi stood also and walked toward the kitchen. She knew in her heart that there was no way that she could leave this house at this point. The problem was finding the courage to tell Greg why she wanted to stay. She wished there was some way to know how he felt. Sometimes she felt their old connection and other times there seemed to be a wall up. There was only one way to find out; she could just be honest and ask him. Then she would know. The thought was terrifying because of the fear of another rejection. After the holidays, she would just have to do it, she decided, but for now, she wanted to just enjoy her time here.

The next few weeks flew by and suddenly it was the week of Thanksgiving. Kevin came home from school on Tuesday all excited from the holiday activities at school. He was wearing a construction paper pilgrim hat and he rattled on for quite some time about all that he had learned about the first Thanksgiving. That evening the three of them were enjoying a spaghetti dinner and both Kevin and Greg were giving her requests for their Thanksgiving favorites. They were all startled when the front doorbell suddenly rang.

"Who could that be?" Lexi asked.

"I don't know," Greg said. "I'll go find out." He stood and went into the living room. A minute later, she heard a lot of laughing and talking. She went into to the room herself just in time to see Greg hugging her sister.

"What are you two doing here?" Lexi asked, hugging Gary and then her sister.

"Aunt Angie!" Kevin called out as he ran into the room.

Angie scooped him up. "Look how you've grown," she said. "I can hardly pick you up."

Kevin giggled and then dropped down and went to hug his Uncle Gary. When all of them finished with their greetings, Lexi looked at her sister and asked, "Why didn't you tell us you were coming?"

"We didn't decide until two days ago," Angie answered, "and we just thought it would be fun to surprise you."

"Did you drive?" Greg asked.

"Yes," Gary answered. "We did it in two days. "It wasn't bad. We drove about ten hours yesterday and we got here around three- thirty this afternoon. We checked into the Waterfront Inn, freshened up, and here we are."

"Have you had dinner?" Lexi asked.

"No," Angie answered. "We were going to offer to take you out for dinner, but something tells me that we are too late. It smells wonderful in here."

"We are having basghetti," Kevin said.

Greg laughed. "We just got started. Please come and join us for basghetti. We have plenty."

They all headed for the kitchen and spent the next hour enjoying their meal and catching up. Gary was very interested in Greg's woodworking business and he offered to give him a hand during his visit. Lexi and Angie talked about their holiday meal. Lexi was excited to have her sister there to help with the baking the next day, especially since Angie had always been far better in the kitchen than she was.

The next day dawned clear and cold. Lexi and Angie made an early run to the grocery to pick up a few items they needed due to the fact that they had made some adjustments to the menu. Later that day, when lunch was over, Gary and Kevin were in the shop with Greg. The two women began mixing ingredients for pies and rolls. After a few moments of quiet work, Angie asked her sister a question about what had been on her mind since their arrival.

"So, what is the situation between you and Greg since you moved in here?" she asked. "I gather that you still have your own room?"

Lexi sighed as she continued peeling apples. "Yes, my room is upstairs. To be honest Ange, I am not sure what our situation is. I know that sounds crazy, but I don't know what else to say."

Angie looked over at Lexi and then looked down and continued to knead dough. "I gather you are no longer trying to 'not be in love with him'. Does he know how you feel about him?"

Lexi shook her head. "I haven't told him because I am so afraid that he will push me away again or completely reject me."

"So...do you plan to just live here forever as his...roommate?"

"No, we agreed to this arrangement through the holidays, then I told him that I would make a decision about where I want to live... and what we are going to do about our marital status." she said. "I don't want to live anywhere else, but I need to be honest with him. I just don't want to risk spoiling Christmas for Kevin if things don't work out."

"On the other hand, wouldn't it be a wonderful Christmas if it did work out?"

Lexi stopped peeling and looked over at her sister but didn't respond.

"Maybe you're just too close to the situation, but it seems simple to me," Angie said. "If I had to guess, he is experiencing the same emotions and fears that you are. You two could waste a lot of time being afraid of the other's reactions. Life is short, you should just go for it. That's my opinion anyway, but you do what you think is best."

Lexi didn't have chance to respond because there was a knock at the back door. It was Kami and Billy. Lexi called Kevin on the intercom and he came in and the two boys were soon upstairs playing. Kami offered to help and soon the three of them were busy working and talking. Angie and Kami made an immediate connection, because both of them loved baking and cooking. Lexi enjoyed those things too, but she didn't have the passion for it that her friend or her sister did.

Eventually, Bill showed up and suddenly plans were made for all for all of them to go out to dinner. Since the next day was Thanksgiving, and they would be eating traditional American food, the decision was made to eat a local restaurant which was well known for its homemade pizza.

As the evening wore on and Lexi found herself thoroughly enjoying the time spent with family and friends, she began to consider her sister's words; "life is short, just go for it". Kami's words a few weeks ago also came back to her, "Are you sure about that?"

Later that night, the Michaels had gone home, Gary and Angie had returned to the Inn, and Kevin was asleep in his room. Lexi was in the kitchen checking on the thawing of the turkey in the refrigerator, when Greg walked in and grabbed a bottle of water, while she had the door open.

"That was fun tonight," he said. "I'm glad that Gary and Angie made the trip. I had almost forgotten how much I like them."

She closed the door and looked up at him. "I'm glad too. I am looking forward to tomorrow."

"So am I," he answered. "They are leaving Saturday morning, right?"

"Right," she answered. "I have been meaning to talk to you about a tree. Kevin and I usually decorate for Christmas the weekend after Thanksgiving. We couldn't do much in our apartment, so I am looking forward to a full-sized tree. What do you think?"

Greg took a swig of his water and then said, "Sure, that sounds good."

"Do you have a tree?" she asked him. He shook his head.

"Do we go real or artificial?"

"We could go and cut one down," he said, "but Bill told me this horror story about having a real one when he was a kid and it caught on fire and burned the house down. They barely got out alive and they lost everything."

"Yeah," she said. "Kami told me about that, and I've known other people that that happened to. Could we maybe get a really nice artificial one?"

"I think we could find some time on Saturday to do that," he told her. "By the way, has Kevin been asking you about going to see Santa Claus? He told me that he has something really important to talk to Santa about, so he thinks that he needs to go see him several times."

"No," Lexi said with surprise. "He hasn't said a word to me about that. What does he want to talk to him about?"

"He wouldn't tell me," Greg answered. "Apparently he thinks if he tells us it will ruin his wish."

"I think he has Christmas mixed up with birthdays," she said. "We need to figure out what he is asking Santa for."

"I know," Greg answered. "At least we have the bike covered, but I don't think that's what this is about."

"Well, let's get through Thanksgiving and then maybe we can figure it out," Lexi said.

"Right," he answered. "I am tired. So, I think I will go to bed. Good night, Lex."

Lexi looked at her husband and the same thoughts that she had had all evening floated through her head.

"Is something wrong?" he asked her as she continued staring at him.

Kevin's Wish

She realized that the door of opportunity had suddenly opened, and she sensed that there was a chance to walk through it. Then her fears clutched at her heart, so she quickly closed it.

She shook her head as if to clear it. "I'm sorry. I was just thinking about the things I have to do in the morning and what time I need to get up. I'll see you in the morning." Then she walked off towards the stairs. She sensed that he was watching her and realized that she probably had sounded foolish just now, but she just couldn't deal with it tonight.

Thanksgiving was more than either Greg or Lexi might have hoped for. The food was delicious, and the time spent together brought all of them a joy that they didn't expect.

On Friday Lexi, Angie and Kami went shopping early. They found a few good bargains and had a nice lunch before returning home to relieve their husbands of the boys.

After enjoying a meal of leftovers, Greg, Lexi and Kevin said good-bye to Gary and Angie, who were leaving early in the morning. Lexi was sad to see them leave. The visit had shown her how much she had missed her sister. When Angie hugged her, she whispered in her ear. *"This is all going to work out. I just know it."*

The words nearly brought tears to her eyes. As she looked up from the hug, she caught Greg watching her and she knew that he sensed that there had been an important exchange between the two of them.

The next day, the three of them went to choose a tree. After searching through three stores, they finally found the perfect one. It was seven feet tall and was covered with hundreds of multicolored lights. After loading up with all kinds of decorations and the new tree, they headed home. While Lexi worked on decorating the inside of the house, Greg and Kevin worked on stringing lights on the deck.

They came in shivering from the cold. The temperature had dropped, and snow was predicted for later that night. Lexi fixed them hot chocolate and turkey sandwiches with the last of the turkey. The rest of the evening was spent decorating the tree to perfection.

When they were finished, Kevin was so tired that he could barely stand up. Greg and Lexi took him upstairs together and tucked him in. Just before he fell asleep, he made a request to see Santa as soon as possible. Lexi asked him what the hurry was. Just before he drifted off to sleep, he murmured something about needing to talk to him about something important.

Over the next two weeks they took him to see a couple of Santa Clauses. The result was the same both times. Kevin sat on Santa's lap and told him a few things he wanted, and then he whispered one last thing in his ear. Afterward, he absolutely refused to discuss it with either of them.

Two weeks later on a Monday afternoon, Lexi went out to the shop to talk to Greg about some of his paperwork. As soon as she opened the door, the smell of polyurethane hit her immediately.

Greg was just putting the finishing touches on a sleigh bed. He looked up and smiled.

"Is this Kami's bed?" she asked.

"Yes," he answered. "It is my very last Christmas project."

"It's beautiful," she told him. She stared at it and then something occurred to her.

"Greg," she began, "I have an idea."

"What's that?" he asked as he stopped working and stood admiring his work for a few minutes.

"When Kami and I were at the flea market a while back, we stopped at a booth that had some beautiful fabrics. There was this one that was blue with white lilies and she fell in love with it. She said that it would make a beautiful bedspread. She almost bought it, but then she got a sad look on her face and said that if she couldn't have her sleigh bed there was no point in her dream bedspread. I had to look sad with her, and it was really hard not to smile."

He stopped looking at the bed and looked over at her. "So, what is your idea?"

"I was thinking about going and getting the fabric and sewing her a bedspread. I have to go to Brookline on Friday for a staff meeting. The flea market isn't far from there. I could go and get it if it's still there; if not, I could hopefully find one close to it. It's Val's birthday too, so I was going to swing by there to drop off a gift, as long as you don't mind me leaving Kevin that long."

"I don't mind," he said. "I do have one question though. You don't have your sewing machine anymore, do you?"

She laughed. "That's the one flaw in my plan," she said. "I thought about getting one at Walmart after I get paid next week."

Greg was thoughtful for a moment and then he asked her a question. "Do you have time to run across town with me? There is something I would like to show you."

"I guess," she answered. "What is it?"

"It will be easier to show you," he said.

Twenty minutes later, Greg parked his truck in front of an empty building in downtown Hull. To her surprise, he pulled some keys out of his pocket and opened the door. The two of them stepped inside and Lexi immediately noticed a large open space with lots of bright light from the large windows. Greg flipped on the light and the room instantly became even brighter. She looked at him questioningly.

"I leased it last summer with an option to buy it within a year," he told her. "My plan was to turn it into a show room for my furniture. I just wasn't sure how I was going to handle building furniture and managing a show room. Then when you moved here and started working with me, I did think that it might become a possibility. I wasn't going to say anything to you until I was sure that you were going to stay in Hull. My plan was to talk to you the first of the year depending on what you decided to do, but just now when you were talking about sewing bedspreads, I had this sudden vision about how good my furniture would look with bedspreads and upholstery. You always were a whiz with a sewing machine. I could buy you a really good heavy duty one and write it off as a business expense." He looked at her. "What do you think?"

"I think it's a wonderful idea," she said, "I do have a question though. I guess it's really none of my business, but I am going to ask anyway." She paused, trying to decide how to phrase the question.

"You seem to be doing quite well financially," she finally said.

Kevin's Wish

A smile spread across his face. "You never did miss much. I guess you have a right to know. When my mother died, Ellen and I learned that she was way more financially sound than either of us knew. That is what Ellen and I had the falling out over. She wanted me to buy a house right down the street from her and live as a cripple and let her take care of me. I bought my house here and made plans to move behind her back. When she found out what I had done and about my new business, she was furious, and she wrote me off as dead. A year later, she moved to North Carolina and I haven't heard from her since."

"That's a shame," Lexi said.

"I guess," Greg told her. "Anyway, the house and shop are paid for and I think I can handle buying this place without a mortgage. That is not my concern. I know that we agreed to wait until after the holidays before we had this conversation, but I would really like to have some idea of what direction you are leaning. The owner had an offer last week from a cash buyer, but I get first option. I need to know if you are interested in becoming involved ...with this business."

Lexi realized that the door was opening again and that she needed to walk through it. She knew that she was staring at him the same way she had in the kitchen a few weeks ago.

"What do you want Lex?" he asked. "I sense a wall up around you at times and other times it seems to come down. Please talk to me without telling me about what's best for Kevin or how you will step aside if I ask you to. What do *you* want?"

There it was; the door was wide open, and he was inviting her to step through it.

She took a breath and began to speak. "I want to stay here in Hull. I want to stay in your house with Kevin and you. The thing is that..." She stopped.

"What?" he asked.

"I don't want to live in your house as your roommate or your housemate. I don't want to be there just as your son's mother or your business partner."

He was staring at her strangely. "I guess I'm not following you," he said.

Lexi could feel her insides trembling. She had come this far, she had to go on.

Kevin's Wish

"I want to live in your house as your wife," she said in a quiet voice. "I love you, Greg. I never stopped loving you, and I probably never will. The thing is that I have not been able to read you either and I don't know where you are on this."

The look on Greg's face could only be explained as utter shock. "Oh Lex," he began, but he was interrupted by the ringing of her cell phone. He stopped and waited as she looked at it.

"It's the school," she said, just before she answered it.

He listened to the one side of her brief conversation, which ended with, "I'll be right there to get him."

Greg's face changed to one of alarm.

"He's sick," she said. "He's running a fever of 102 and he says that his throat feels like it's on fire."

"Let's go," he said.

They were at the school within ten minutes. They took him straight to an urgent care where he was diagnosed with strep throat. The doctor gave him a shot and a prescription for some antibiotics. He said that he would be fine in a few days, but that they needed to make sure that his fever didn't spike too high.

Lexi had been through this before. She knew that the doctor was right. Kevin would be fine in a few days. She did realize that it would be a long few days. Greg, however, suddenly became a nervous parent. Lexi found it heartwarming to see him constantly checking on him and forcing the fluids. It didn't seem as stressful when she wasn't the only one caring for him.

With their concerns about their son, the conversation they were having in the downtown store, seemed to be shelved. Lexi wasn't sure about Greg's reaction to her proclamation of love, so her wall went up again and the subject was closed once more.

By Thursday night, Kevin was fever free. He was still tired and catching up on sleep, and he hadn't regained all of his appetite. Greg had also seemed to recover from his parental anxiety. He insisted that she should stick to her original plan for Friday of going to her staff meeting and taking Val her birthday present. He didn't mention buying the fabric for Kami's bedspread. She decided that he must have left that up to her.

Kevin's Wish

As she was preparing to leave the next morning, Greg stopped her.

"You do know that there is heavy snow predicted for tonight, don't you?" he asked.

"Yes," she said. "I should be back by eight or so. I think it is supposed to start around ten or eleven isn't it?"

"As of now, yes. I just hope it doesn't change," he said.

She smiled at him. "I'll be fine," she told him, "but thanks for caring." As she opened the door and stepped out, he spoke one more time.

"I do care, Lex."

Chapter Five

It was three o'clock in the afternoon before Lexi left the newspaper office in Brookline. The sky had a snowy grey look to it and the temperature had dropped dramatically. She decided that she needed to make her way to the flea market and take care of her business as quickly as possible.

To her delight, the fabric that Kami had fallen in love with was still available in the same booth where they had seen it before. She made the purchase quickly and made her way back to her car. There wasn't much of a crowd today, probably due to the cold and to the pending snow, so her entire mission didn't take long.

Kevin's Wish

Forty minutes later, she was at the Fletcher's house delivering Val's birthday gift. They invited her to stay for dinner, but as she looked out the window at the increasingly dark skies, something told her that she needed to get started on her trip home. She declined their invitation, explaining that Kevin had been sick, and she felt that he needed to get home to check on him.

Shortly after leaving, she called Greg and told him that she was on her way home.

"Be careful," he told her. "The forecast has changed. The storm is moving in much sooner than expected."

"I am seeing a few flakes of snow," she said, "but it isn't bad."

"I'm glad," he said, "But if it does pick up just slow down."

"I will," she answered. Then after a minute, she said, "Damn."

"What's wrong?" he asked.

"I think the heater on my car has gone out again. I paid a guy three hundred and fifty dollars to fix it last year."

He sighed. She had no way of knowing what he was thinking, but it couldn't be good."

"Lex?" he asked.

"What?"

"Please be careful. I...what is that beeping sound?"

Now she sighed. "My phone is about to die," she told him.

"Can't you put it on the charger?"

She looked down at the place where her charger should be. It was empty. Then she remembered that she had put her charger in his truck when they had gone to the mall the weekend before. She vaguely remembered seeing it on the kitchen counter. He had apparently brought it in, and she had made a mental note several times to put it back in her car. Obviously, that had never happened.

"Greg?" she asked. There was no response. She looked down at her phone. It was dead. She was alone and suddenly the snow started coming down harder. She was completely alone and cut off from the world.

Kevin's Wish

Back at the house in Hull, Greg was frantically repeating her name.

"Lex?"

"Lex, are you there?"

"Lex?"

Suddenly he looked down at the counter and saw her car charger where he had put it four days ago. Lexi was driving into a snowstorm, in a car with no heat and a dead cell phone. There was nothing he could do about it because his son was upstairs recovering from strep throat. He was just going to have to wait it out.

An hour passed and his anxiety was growing. Under normal conditions, she should be home by now. He looked outside and saw the snow was now coming down hard and fast, and blowing nearly sideways.

Thirty minutes later, he called Bill and explained the situation to him. He asked him if he would come over and stay at the house if he decided to go out and look for her. Bill told him that he would happy to help out, but he encouraged him to wait at least another thirty minutes before going out. He could easily miss her and then she would be home worried about him, so Greg agreed to wait a little while longer.

After another thirty minutes had passed, Greg picked up his phone and prepared to call Bill back as he began to walk toward the mud room to get his boots. Just as he leaned over to pick up his boots, he heard the sound of the garage door opening. He quickly opened the door to the garage and watched as Lexi stopped her car and the overhead door began to go down. He rushed out and opened the driver's door of her car and saw her sitting with her head on the steering wheel.

"Lex, are you all right?" he asked.

After a few seconds, she looked up and spoke softly. "I'm so cold."

"Come on," he said, "let's get you warmed up."

He reached down and took her hand and gently pulled her out of the car. Inside of the house, he helped her take her coat off and then he wrapped his arms around her tightly and held her close. He wasn't sure if that was for her benefit or his, but it didn't matter. They stood that way quietly for a few minutes and then he let go of her and led her into the living room. After settling her on the couch, he pulled a blanket off the back of the couch and wrapped it around her.

"Can I get you something?" he asked. "Are you hungry?"

"I am very hungry," she told him, "but I think I would like to take a nice hot shower first."

"That's a good idea," he told her. "Why don't you use my shower. Kevin was much better this evening. He ate a really good dinner and he is sleeping pretty soundly."

"All right," she answered, too tired to argue. "I'll just run up and get a few things. I'll be quiet."

"I'll start fixing you something to eat," he said.

A few minutes later, Lexi was standing in Greg's extra-large walk-in shower enjoying the blissfully hot water pouring over her. She stayed there until she was just too exhausted to stand there any longer.

A short time later, she came into the living room where Greg was setting up a TV tray with leftovers from the dinner that he and Kevin had shared earlier. She was impressed. There was two chicken legs, macaroni and cheese, and green beans.

"You cooked this, all by yourself?" she asked.

He smiled. "I have learned some skills over the last few years."

She ate quietly for a few minutes and when she finished, Greg took the plate to the kitchen and then put away the TV tray.

Feeling another chill coming on, she wrapped the quilt back around her and melted into the couch. She yawned just as Greg sat down and looked at her. She waited for him to say something about her irresponsibility in not making sure that her phone was charged or in forgetting to put the charger back in her car, but he didn't say a word.

She soon felt herself drifting off to sleep. The thought crossed her mind that she should get up and go up to her room, but then she was feeling warm and comfy, so she didn't move.

Kevin's Wish

A few times during the night, she felt a small chill, but then just as quickly, she would warm right back up.

When she woke, she was confused, because she wasn't sure where she was. After looking around, she realized that she was in Greg's room and in his bed. She sat up and looked around and realized that she was alone. According to the clock by the bed, it was eight-forty-five.

Then, in a flash the events of the night before came back to her; the frightening drive home in the snow, Greg's concern over her, taking a shower, and then falling asleep on the couch.

The throw from the couch was on the bed, so she grabbed it and wrapped it around herself before she walked out into the kitchen. There she found Greg sitting at the table, drinking coffee and reading the newspaper.

"Good morning," he said, when he noticed her standing there. "How are you feeling?"

She smiled at him and walked toward the coffee. "I'm fine," she told him. After she filled her cup, she walked over and sat across from him and looked at him.

"Couple of questions," she began. "How did I end up in your bed?"

"You fell asleep on the couch," he told her. "I thought it seemed cold in the living room. I was concerned about how cold you had been earlier, so I carried you to my bed. With my leg, I didn't think I could carry you up to your room, so that's why you were in my bed. Next question."

"What?" she asked.

"You said that you had a couple of questions. What else did you want to know?"

Lexi stared at her coffee while she stirred the spoon around idly in it.

"I started to sleep on the couch, but I couldn't get comfortable, so I came into the bedroom and slept in my bed." He grinned. "We *are* married after all, but nothing happened."

She smiled. "I think I would have remembered that."

"Lex," Greg began, "last week when the school called about Kevin, we were in the middle of a conversation."

Lexi clenched her coffee cup a little harder. "Yes, we were," she said.

"Things got a little crazy around here," he told her, "but I..."

She looked up from her coffee cup. "Greg, I know my declaration of love caught you off guard, but I have realized how I felt almost from the moment I saw you at the wedding. I tried to deny it to myself, but I just couldn't. I held back from letting you know because I am just so afraid of being rejected by you again."

He sighed and reached out and took her hand. "I understand that completely. I'm glad you were honest with me. I love you too, Lex. I've never lost my feelings for you. I love you more than you will ever know, but I have my own fears."

"What?" she asked in a soft voice. "Please talk to me."

"I am afraid," he began, "that if we get back together, everything will be fine for a while and then eventually you will start to want a whole man. That would be more painful down the road, than it would be if you rejected me now."

She stared at him for a moment before she spoke. "So, we're right back where we were six years ago in your hospital room?"

"I'm not going to send you away, Lex. I'm just caught up in my fears and I'm not sure what to do," he told her.

As she stared at her husband, Lexi's heart began to feel lighter. She had a sudden realization that everything was going to be all right. Six years earlier she had allowed him to push her away. There was no way that she was going to make that mistake again.

"Mom," Kevin said as he bounded into the room. "You're home. I am all better and I was hoping we could make some Christmas cookies. You don't have to go to any meetings today, do you?"

Lexi smiled at her son. "No, honey. I'm not going anywhere. I'm staying right here." As she spoke, she squeezed Greg's hand. She then stood up and walked toward the refrigerator. "What do you want for breakfast?"

"Bacon and eggs," Kevin said with a delighted smile on his face.

Kevin's Wish

The next day Greg and Lexi took their son to see Santa one last time before Christmas. Since they had told him that this was the last time, the child decided to make the most of it. After they waited in line at the mall for over thirty minutes, Kevin climbed onto Santa's lap and began to immediately have a whispered conversation with him. Santa leaned down and spoke softly to him for a moment and whatever he said, made Kevin's face light up. He responded with a few quick words that Lexi was pretty sure were, "Thank you". Then he jumped down and walked back to his parents, who had given up on asking him what he was talking to Santa about.

"All done?" Greg asked.

"Yes," Kevin answered. "Can we go to the pet shop now? I want to look at the puppies." He didn't wait for a reply, but just turned around and started walking, assuming that his parents would follow.

Greg and Lexi exchanged a look and read each other's minds. They now knew what his wish was. He wanted a puppy for Christmas. As he continued to walk away from them, they had no choice but to follow him.

Inside the store, Kevin went straight to the puppy section and stopped in front of a beagle. He held an extended conversation with the dog telling him what a "good boy" he was. Then he looked around and spotted an Irish Setter. Moving to his cage, he had the same conversation with that dog. When he finished, he turned around and said, "I'm hungry. Can we get something to eat now?"

Lexi was speechless. What exactly was Kevin up to? Was this little show supposed to let them know his choice of dogs? She looked at Greg who was trying not to smile too much.

On the way home, they made another stop, to Lexi's surprise. Thirty minutes later, she was the proud owner of a very expensive heavy-duty sewing machine.

"Should I consider this a Christmas present?" she asked.

"If you want to consider it that you can," he answered with a smile. "but I am going to consider it a business write off."

Lexi smiled. They hadn't continued their conversation from the morning before. She hoped that the purchase of this sewing machine was a sign that Greg realized that she wasn't going anywhere.

Later that night, after Kevin was asleep, the two of them discussed the situation.

"I don't have a problem with him having a pet," Greg said. "It's a good way for him to learn responsibility. I just think that it would make a better birthday present because the weather would be better to house train a dog."

"I would agree," Lexi told him, "but how do we handle the Santa situation?"

"Do you think that Santa told him he could have one?" Greg asked.

"That's exactly what I mean," she answered. "He walked away from Santa lit up like a Christmas tree."

He was thoughtful for a moment. "Let's not get too worked up about this. We'll figure something out."

"All right," she said. "We have plenty of other things to deal with without stressing about this." As soon as the words were out of her mouth, she realized what Greg probably thought she meant. She looked at him and saw that he was looking at her thoughtfully.

"I didn't mean..."

He smiled. "I know you didn't. What day next week is Kevin's Christmas program?"

"Did he just change the subject?" Lexi wondered. "It is Wednesday afternoon," she said, "at two o'clock."

A quiet moment followed before Lexi said, "I am excited about the sewing machine. I want to get started on Kami's comforter right away. Can you help me get it set up tomorrow?"

"Absolutely," he answered. "I'll bring it in from the truck right after Kev gets on the bus. Where do you want it?"

She thought for a moment. "Ideally, my room would be the best place, because it would be out of the way. I don't think that we want the mess in the living room, but on the other hand, I think that it would be hard to haul upstairs."

"Oh definitely," he answered. "I have an idea. I think I can fix up a corner of my shop for you to have a sewing area. How would you feel about that?"

A smile crossed her face. Another sign that he was planning on her staying here.

"I think that's an excellent idea," she answered. Suddenly her sister's words of almost a month ago, echoed in her head. "Just go for it." She considered the possibility of making a move toward him, but there was still a small amount of fear in her, so she backed off the idea. She told him good-night and a few minutes later, she was in bed excited about the idea of sewing again.

It was nearly noon the next day, before Greg came in from the shop and told her that he had her sewing room ready. She had just returned from shopping for sewing supplies. After following him to the shop, she was amazed at what he had accomplished in a few short hours. He had partitioned off an area with plywood and had built a table for the machine. He moved a small desk in from somewhere. Not only that, he had nailed several shelves to the wall. The wood was all unfinished, but he promised that they could paint or stain it after the holidays.

"Greg, this is just unbelievable," she said, trying not to choke up.

The expression on his face showed that he was pleased by her reaction.

"Well, I am going to leave you to your sewing," he told her. "I have some things I need to take care of in town."

"Where are you going?" she asked.

He walked toward the door and then turned around. "That's none of your business," he said with a smile. Then he walked out of the shop without another word.

Christmas Eve day arrived faster than Lexi imagined that it could have. Greg and Lexi planned the day to make it exciting and fun for Kevin. Bill and Kami were leaving at three o'clock to go to her parents' home in New Bedford along with Aunt Gracie, who would be coming back and spending the night with them. As soon as Greg received a text from Bill that they were gone, he called a couple of the students that worked for him and they came over to help him load Kami's sleigh bed.

Kevin's Wish

An hour later, when the bed was assembled, Lexi made up the bed, then spread out the new comforter and set up the pillow shams. When she finished, the two of them stood back to admire their work.

"This is Billy's mom's big surprise?" Kevin asked.

"Yes," Kami answered. "Isn't it nice?"

Kevin frowned. "It doesn't seem like a very exciting surprise to me."

Greg laughed. "Son, you have a lot to learn about women."

"It is absolutely beautiful," Lexi said.

"Do you think you would ever want a bed like this?" Greg asked her.

She thought for a moment. "I'm not sure. You would need the right room for a bed this size. This bedroom is huge, so it is perfect for a large bed." She thought for a moment and eyed the doors on the other side of the room. A grin came across her face. "I am going to be nosy. I just can't help myself. Then she walked across the room and opened one of the doors.

After laughing, she said, "Just as I thought; a massive walk in closet."

"Can we go now?" Kevin asked. "We need to make more cookies for Santa, because Dad ate all of the last ones we made."

"*Dad* ate them all?" Greg asked.

Kevin got a funny look on his face. "Well, maybe Dad didn't eat all of them, but anyway we need to make more. Can we go?"

"All right," Kami laughed, ruffling her son's head. "Let's go."

Later that night, the three of them sat in the living room, with the lights turned off, admiring the tree. Kevin finished arranging the cookies on a plate on the coffee table and then he curled up between his parents on the couch. Lexi could tell that he was getting sleepy, so she thought that it wouldn't be long before they could put him to bed.

They were all quiet for a moment and then Greg spoke up. "I have an idea. Why don't we all open just one present tonight?"

Kevin's Wish

Lexi was a little surprised, but before she could respond, Kevin jumped up and said. "Can I go first?"

Greg laughed. "Go ahead."

Kevin ran to the back of the tree and picked out a gift that he apparently had been eyeing. It was a long thin gift that he opened very quickly. He smiled and held up the very grownup looking fishing pole. "Dad, did you pick this out for me?"

Greg smiled at his son. "Yes, I did." Kevin jumped on his father's lap and gave him a big hug. Lexi watched holding back her tears. After a minute, Kevin jumped up and grabbed another present from under the tree. It was small square package which he handed to his father.

Kevin watched as his father opened the watch that he had chosen for him. Then there was another hug followed by a moment of silence.

"I guess it's Mom's turn, isn't it?" Kevin asked.

"I guess so," Greg answered.

Lexi stared at the tree and the gifts, not sure what to pick. Suddenly Greg spoke up. "I think there is something stuck under the couch.

Then he reached down and pulled out a box. He looked at it for a moment and then handed it to Lexi who was confused.

"Aren't you going to open it?" Kevin asked.

"I guess I should," she said and began pulling off the wrapping paper. Inside was a square white box. She took the lid off and gasped.

Kevin slid across the couch to her and looked at the box. "What is it?" he asked.

"Well, son, let me explain this to you," Greg began. "When your mother and I were married, we didn't have a lot of money to buy wedding rings. I was getting ready to ship out to Afghanistan, so we decided to wait until I got back to buy our rings. I was gone a lot longer than we planned and it took a long time for me to recover from losing my leg. Anyway, now that we are all here together, I think it is time that we wear wedding rings to show the world that we are going to be together forever."

Lexi looked up at Greg. "You remembered."

He smiled. "I didn't at first, but when I was in the first jewelry store that I went to, it seemed to come back to me in a flash. Then I remembered which store we saw those rings in. That is what I was doing in Boston last week. I went to that store and found the ring you wanted. I think it is a slightly different style, but it's pretty close."

He reached over and pulled the diamond studded wedding ring out of the box. "May I?" he asked.

Tears were flowing freely down her face now, and she silently nodded. He took her hand and slid the ring onto her finger. She looked at it for a few seconds and then she pulled the other ring out of the box. Still without speaking a word, she slid the gold ring on his finger.

Kevin, who had been quietly watching the entire exchange between the two of them, asked a question.

"Does this mean we are all going to live here together forever?"

Kevin looked at his son. "It means that we are a family and we will all live together as a family, at least until you grow up, but your mother and I will be together always."

"Are you going to have more kids?" Kevin asked. "I would really like a little brother."

Greg looked over at Lexi and she smiled through her tears. "I would say that is a very good possibility at some point down the road," he answered.

Then Kevin jumped up and starting dancing around the room, talking in a sing song voice. "Thank you, thank you, Santa."

Greg and Lexi stared at their son in confusion. "Why are you thanking Santa?" Lexi asked.

"That's what I have been asking him for," Kevin answered. "I wanted us to be a real family, like Billy is with his mom and dad. I wanted you two to be in love like Bill and Kami. They are always hugging and kissing, and they share the same room. I wanted a family like that, so I asked Santa as many times as I could, and it worked."

"You weren't asking him for a puppy?" Greg asked.

"Of course not," Kevin answered. "You can't ask Santa for a puppy. It's not safe for him to carry them on the sled. Everybody knows that. Dad don't you think that you should kiss Mom now?"

Kevin's Wish

Still reeling from the worldliness of his son's statements, Greg smiled and said, "I think maybe I should." Then he moved over closer to his wife and pulled her into his arms and began to kiss her. As he kissed her, Lexi felt a sense of joy and peace that she had not felt in a long time. It was like coming home. After a moment they were pulled out of their emotional embrace, by the sound of their son saying, "Ok, that's enough."

They both laughed and Greg looked down and said, "My new watch says that it is time for you to go to bed. The sooner you get to sleep, the sooner it will be Christmas morning."

Kevin reluctantly agreed and within thirty minutes, he was sound asleep. Back downstairs in the living room, Greg took Lexi in his arms and kissed her again. After a moment, he pulled away and smiled down at her.

"Before this goes any further, we probably better take care of our Santa duties. I should go over to the neighbors and collect Kevin's gifts."

"Greg," Lexi said, as she continued to hold him tightly, "did something happen that helped you move past your fears?"

He looked down at her as he answered her question. "I think it was the morning that we were talking, and you told Kevin that you weren't going anywhere; you were staying right here. There was a look in your eye that told me that you weren't going to give up on me. Then I had a sudden feeling that everything was going to be all right. I still have some fears hidden away, but it fades away whenever I see that you are still here. I love you Lex."

"I made the mistake of running away once and I'm not going to do that again," she told him. "You are stuck with me now," she grinned.

He smiled back at her and kissed her again. "I better get going," he said. "I'll be back shortly."

"All right," she told him. "I'll stay here."

Greg returned about thirty minutes later, with a smile on his face. "Bill and Kami are right behind me. She wants to thank you for the comforter. She is beside herself with excitement."

"Where is Billy?" Lexi frowned and then answered her own question. "Oh, Aunt Gracie is there."

Kevin's Wish

At that moment, Bill and Kami knocked on the side door. When Lexi opened it, she was nearly knocked over by Kami's bear hug.

"The comforter is beautiful! I can't believe you went back and found that material. That was so thoughtful. I just...Greg said you had something to show us. What?"

Lexi smiled and looked up at Greg. He put his arm around her and pulled her closer. Then Lexi held up her hand for the other two to see her ring.

"Oh Lexi, that's beautiful! Did Greg give you that tonight?"

She nodded. "It's the ring that we picked out years ago. We couldn't afford it when we got married, so we were going to buy it when he got back from his deployment, then well...you know, so he went hunting for it last week and luckily he found it."

"Oh, that's so special," Kami said with a hint of a tear in her eye. She turned and looked at her own husband. "I guess we are both lucky women, aren't we?"

"You are," Bill said in answer to his wife's question. "Now I think it's time that we wish our friends a very Merry Christmas and be on our way."

"Merry Christmas," Greg said pulling his wife a little closer.

"Merry Christmas," Bill, Kami, and Lexi all chimed at once.

A moment later, Greg and Lexi were alone, and they began to set up Kevin's Santa Claus haul. The last thing they did was place the bicycle against the wall next to the tree. They stood admiring the scene for a moment. Then Greg looked over at her and asked, "Is there anything else we need to do tonight?"

"Not that I can think of," she said. "I think I am just about ready for bed. How about you?"

He smiled and reached up and switched off the living room light. "I'm ready too." He reached over and put his arm around her. After leaning down and kissing her, he said, "Welcome Home." Then the two of them walked to their room arm in arm.

Epilogue

Three years later

Lexi had just turned on the microwave to reheat spaghetti for lunch, when she heard Kevin yell, "Mom!"

She sighed, tuned around and walked into the living room. Kevin was standing at the bottom of the stairs and pointing. She walked over to him and looked at the stairs. Her eighteen-month-old daughter had climbed halfway up the stairs.

"Did you lift her over the gate?" she asked.

"No," Kevin said. "I think she climbed over it when I was in the bathroom."

Lexi opened the gate and moved up the steps and grabbed the child. "Kerry, no!" she scolded as she carried her down the stairs and closed the gate back. "Where is your sister?"

At that point, there was a crash in the corner as little Kelly pulled over a potted plant. The noise scared her, and she began to cry, which triggered Kerry to begin crying also. At that exact moment, the microwave began beeping and demanding attention.

Lexi and Kevin looked at each and then they both began to laugh, probably because there was nothing else to do at that point. "I think it's time to eat," she told him. She shifted Kerry to her hip and picked up Kelly and put her on her other hip.

Ten minutes later, Greg walked into the kitchen. The twins were in their highchairs and their faces were covered with spaghetti. Kevin was about to refill his plate, and Lexi was grabbing bites between helping the girls get some of the food into their mouths.

"Hey," he said. "Who wants some good news?"

"I would love some," Lexi said. "Is it about the new house?"

Greg grinned and held up a set of keys. "The contractor finished this morning. I did a walk through with him. Everything looked good. If you can get away later this afternoon, you can do your own walk through and he is going to meet us at four o'clock to sign the final papers."

Lexi smiled at her husband. "Does that mean that we can move in?"

"Yes, it does," he answered.

"That's good, because just a little while ago, little miss climber vaulted over the gate and got halfway up the stairs."

Greg grinned and put his hand on Kerry's head. "Well, my little gymnast won't have any stairs to climb in the new house."

Lexi looked at her daughter. "I'm sure she will find something else to climb on."

"Without a doubt," he answered.

"I am going to have some spaghetti and then I need to run some errands in town, unless you need my help here," he said.

"No, I don't need anything," she said, "The twins are going down for a nap right after lunch, but thanks for asking."

"You are very welcome," he told her as he leaned to down to give her a kiss.

Kevin rolled his eyes and then asked, "Dad, can I go with you?"

Greg looked at his son and completely understood his need to get out of the house. "You sure can," he answered. Then as he started to walk toward the cabinet for a plate, he glanced into the living room.

"Honey, did you know that there is a plant turned over in the living room and there is dirt everywhere?"

Kevin and Lexi looked at each other and began laughing again.

Other Books by Debbie Williams:

Daring Set

Daring to Hope – 2014

Daring to Love – 2015

Rocky Mountain Way - 2015

Kate's Journey Home – 2015

Living and Loving in Arizona Series

Tara's Legend – 2016

Sarah's Family – 2017

Friends in the Fold – 2017

Living in the Fold – 2018

Weddings and Funerals -2018

Ryan's Daughters – 2019

Coming in 2020:

Losing Warren

Made in the USA
Monee, IL
15 December 2020